Hunting Holly

by **Karin Hedges**

Page layout and book design by Armchair ePublishing, Anacortes, WA
Cover Design ©Tony D. Locke, Armchair ePublishing
Image of fabric swatch used on front and back cover used with
permission from MJ Trends. www.mjtrends.com

Dedication

I would like to dedicate this book to my friends and family. Thank you so much for your support.

Acknowledgments

First of all I would like to thank my biggest fan, my brother Michael. Had it not been for his encouragement and enthusiasm I would never have put any of this story to paper. His passion and support kept me from walking away from the project all together. He read over countless drafts and was always willing to listen when I needed to bounce ideas off someone. He pushed me to be a better writer. Secondly I would like to thank my sister Kristin, whose encouragement gave me the confidence to keep writing. Her honesty and brilliant perspective sent me back to the drawing board more than once, but the end result was always worth it. I want to thank my dedicated group of editors who had to wait for the manuscript chapter by chapter. I also would like to thank Armchair ePublishing. Tony and Karla Locke's patience, wisdom and talent made this book possible. Finally I would like to thank all the friends and family who supported this book.

Preface

Two black figures dropped catlike to the ground from an apartment fire escape, landing side by side in a dark alley. Both wore tight-fitting, black clothes with black gloves and balaclavas. They had slim, black, weighted packs strapped tight across their backs. Together, they took off at a sprint, down the alley, and into the night.

They ran through the sleeping city, jumping off buildings, hurtling over low walls, and flipping over every obstacle. It would have been amazing to watch had anybody seen, but they slipped through the shadows undetected. They broke into a dead sprint when they entered into a small park. The black clad pair raced under a small bridge and pulled up short. The first pulled off his mask and panted heavily.

"Nice try, Holly, but I was faster," he gasped between breaths. He had short dark brown hair, chocolate colored eyes and tanned skin. He was young, only seventeen. Even under his thin jacket his muscles were obvious.

"No way, Matt, I won! Plus, I was quieter," replied Holly, breathing just as hard. She pulled off her mask revealing pale blond hair pulled up in a loose pony tail. She was a little younger than Matt. Her muscles were a little more subtle, leaner. She grinned and her bright blue eyes scanned the surroundings.

"You both lose," said a voice behind them.

Matt and Holly spun around to face the newcomer. A light sparked to life, illuminating the three of them.

"You both failed to watch your surroundings and each other's backs; a lesson I have tried to teach you. Clearly, I have not done an adequate job." The speaker was holding a flashlight and wore a stern look on his face. He was clean shaven and his black hair was cut short; he was older, in his 30's. He was also dressed in dark and unmemorable clothes.

"Sorry, Nick. It won't happen again," said the teens in unison.

"Now tonight, we're going to work on sparring. You know your first real mission is coming up soon, and it's my job to make sure you are prepared for whatever may come," he told them.

The three trained in the dark park for several hours before Matt and Holly returned to the small apartment building they both lived in. Instead of going inside, they climbed up the fire escape and sat side by side on the flat roof where they talked for most of the night. Matt and Holly were closer to each other than anyone else they knew. They both lived alone in the same apartment building (despite their age, but nobody knew that little detail), they both went to the same school, and they both worked for the same mysterious and nameless group. They were best friends and partners for the past three years. A few hours before dawn, they climbed into their own small apartment rooms. Holly crawled in through the window that was always left unlocked.

The apartment was totally black. Something moved in the room, and she felt a heavy blow to the back of her head. Holly hit the floor and blacked out.

Chapter 1

Riding in the trunk of a car, handcuffed, is not one of my favorite forms of transportation. In fact, it's usually one of those moments where you stop and ponder whether this job is really worth it. Unfortunately, I have those moments rather often. What I hate more than riding in the trunk of a car handcuffed, is waking up in said car and not remembering how I got there. Not only is it uncomfortable, it's also unnerving.

Rolling over, I quickly searched the trunk for anything useful and found that I was the only occupant in the trunk. I switched my hands in front of me. Sounds easy enough, but it's a tricky thing to do when in the confined space of a car trunk. When I had that accomplished, I braced myself against the inside of the trunk and with both feet, I kicked where the tail lights were located. Nothing happened at first, but after repeating the move, I heard the bulb break. With a broken tail light, a cop might see it and pull the car over, but not very likely. Silently praying my kidnapper had not heard me, I slipped off my shoe and pulled a lock pick from the sole. I quickly loosened the handcuffs, so it would appear that I was still bound, but I could twist out of them. I set to work on opening the trunk from the inside. From the speed of the car and the lack of turns it was making, I assumed we were on the highway. Suddenly, the car made a sharp turn and started to slow down. Since the car was probably taking an off-ramp, I needed to work fast if I was to get out of this mess. The emergency release lever was disconnected, it was hopeless. But I would be stupid not to try it. Next, I jammed the pick into the lock and tried to pop it open, but that did not work either.

The car slammed to a halt, and I hit the inside of the trunk, hard.

I will definitely be feeling that tomorrow. Then I jerked to the left as the car drove on. I started to panic, "What will happen if I can't get out of the trunk? Where were my captors taking me?" I thought. The car turned a few more times, and the sounds of traffic faded. It seemed they were taking me to somewhere isolated. The car slammed to a stop, but I braced myself against the side this time. I heard the car doors open, then close, and I scrambled to adjust the cuffs, making them loose so I could pull my hands out quickly.

The trunk popped open and I tensed my body, preparing for the blow that I knew was coming. The larger of the two men stood over me and punched me in the face, and my head reeled a little. I could taste blood in my mouth. He grabbed a fist full of hair and dragged me out of the trunk onto the ground. The smaller one had a small hand gun and stood just out of arms reach. My eyes flicked back to the larger man just in time to see his fist pull back and steeled myself for the blow. The hit almost knocked the wind out of me, almost. I kicked as hard as I could at the larger one's knee and put all my weight behind it. At the same time, I twisted out of the loose handcuffs. The man's knee bent backwards and made a sickening crunch as it broke. He let me go, fell to the ground and screamed. I spun around to meet the smaller one, who raised his gun to shoot. I grabbed his wrist and pointed it away from me, twisting his wrist with a sharp jerk. I spun under his arm and broke it over my shoulder. He dropped the gun and I kicked it away, rolling into a judo throw. He landed in front of me, on his back. I straightened out of the throw and stomped on his forehead, which knocked him out.

My cell phone had fallen out of his pocket and I picked it up along with the handcuffs and gun. I spit out some blood from my mouth and glanced around at my surroundings for the first time, realizing I was standing in front of an abandoned warehouse surrounded by woods. To the east and a little farther down the only road in sight were a few small old houses. Sadly, it looked like nobody was home. The smaller guy was down for the count, but the larger was trying to get up. He held a small knife in his hand. I opened the handcuffs, kicked the knife out of his hand, and kicked him back to the ground. I handcuffed him to the chain link fence next to him. I cocked the gun and looked down at his face, contorted with pain.

"Who are you?" I asked simply.

"You bitch," he spat at me, then screamed as I stepped on his broken knee.

"Who are you and why did you kidnap me?" I asked again.

"I'm Markus and he paid us," he spat through gritted teeth.

"That's better. Now who is 'he'?" I asked.

"That's Garret," he said looking at his companion lying on muddy gravel ground a few feet away.

"No, I don't really care about him. I mean the man that paid you to grab me."

"Go to hell," he snarled. I put more pressure on his knee and rotated my foot a little. "Okay, okay, I'll tell you! I don't know who he is, just a voice on the phone. We get a package with a picture, place, and time," he replied.

"And you were supposed to bring me here?" I asked.

"Yes, then we call him for instructions," he gasped as I ground my foot into his knee. "That's all I know, I swear!" he cried.

"Was I the only person you two were told to grab?" I asked, slightly lifting my foot off his knee.

"No, a boy too, but that's all! His picture is in the car," he said quickly.

I walked to the car and opened the door. It was cluttered with papers and old food. I found a ziplock bag with the contents of my pockets from before I was grabbed. I picked up the pile of papers on the dashboard. The stack included several pictures of me as well as notes on my weekly schedule; it was unsettling how much they knew. I came to the last picture and it was not of me. It took me a second to figure out who it was, because it was so blurred. I gasped and dropped it. It fluttered to the gravel ground and landed face up. It was Matt, my best friend.

I pulled open my phone and pressed the speed dial. The phone rang for a few seconds, but it felt like an eternity. Finally, it was answered by a brisk feminine voice.

"Holly? Where the hell are you? What happened? You sent a distress signal and we came right over, but all we found was your empty apartment. Report and make it fast."

"Tonya, I have a problem here. Long story short. I was kidnapped and brought to some warehouse. I incapacitated the kidnappers and found that they were also supposed to grab Matt," I reported.

"I need more to work with than that, kid."

"Two guys, both down. One with a broken leg and the other… let's just say he is not going to wake up anytime soon. I also have one handgun and one car with a little gas. They were supposed to call their boss for more info. A few houses, a couple blocks away, might be a safe place to get more supplies." I ran through the report and read the address off the side of the warehouse.

"That's more like it. I'm pulling up your current location on the computer now and it looks like there is a gas station about two miles east. I can have a team sent to clean up the mess in a half hour. Force them to make the call and get all the info on who this guy is, then shoot the two and walk to the gas station. Clean yourself up and wait for a ride, I'm sending someone now," she ordered.

"What! Kill them? I can't do that!" I gasped.

"Sure you can, just pull the trigger and hide the bodies 'til my men get there." said Tonya.

"I'm no killer," I said quietly.

"Look, Holly, you knew what you were getting into when you joined us. Sometimes the ends justify the means. In this case, that means shooting the kidnappers. You don't get to pick and choose what you do when you work for us; it's all or nothing."

"I have another idea. If this doesn't work, I'll knock them out and hide them. Then you guys can do the rest." I hung up before she could protest and set to work.

I dragged the smaller one, evidently named Garret, into the passenger side of the car. That was the easy part, even though he easily weighed sixty pounds more than me. The hard part would be the call. Reaching into Garret's pocket, I pulled out his cell phone and shut the door. I walked back to Markus, flipped open the phone, and started searching for the right number.

"I am going to call your friend, and you get to tell him you have me. Then, you get to ask what to do next, and whatever I tell you to say," I informed a rather pissed-off Markus.

"Why should I?" he spat.

I raised the gun back to his temple, "Because I have this. Now just a few rules before we get started. First, no tip-offs. You really don't want him to know anything I don't want him to know. If you know what I mean. Secondly, no screaming in pain or anything like that. We don't want him to know your plan did not work out. Lastly, don't do anything stupid. If you behave you might just live through this. Agreed?"

He nodded his head.

"Great, now what's the number?"

I dialed in the number that he rattled off from memory.

Thirty minutes later, I walked up to the gas station. It felt good to have my stuff back: my wallet, cell, knife, and other knick-knacks I always carried. I went into the bathroom on the side of the building first. It probably wasn't a good idea to walk into a store looking like I just fought for my life and covered in someone else's blood. I cleaned up in the sink, but there was little to do for some of the cuts and bruises. Inside the gas station store, I bought a water bottle, ham sandwich, and small first aid kit. I handed the clerk cash as he tried not to stare. With my new items, I walked back to the bathroom and cleaned up the cuts as best I could. My face wasn't too bad, but my hand had a gash that wouldn't stop bleeding. I wrapped it up and sat by the bus stop, waiting for the ride Tonya said she was sending. I didn't have to wait too long; about twenty minutes later, a black SUV pulled up. The tinted window rolled down showing a platinum blond woman of about forty.

"I'm Jessica. My orders are to get you to the Local Command Center," she said simply.

That was good enough for me. I climbed in.

We drove through most of the night. After hours of back roads, I had no idea where we were or where we were going. After a few hours in the dark, I could feel the adrenaline fade out of my bloodstream. I hadn't slept since the night before, not counting the ride in the trunk. I was tired, but I couldn't sleep. Every time I closed my eyes, I saw the faces of Markus and Garret. I knew Tonya wanted me to kill them, but I couldn't. She would not be happy with me, but I stopped two unnecessary killings. They didn't deserve to die, they were just following orders. I saved them, but that didn't mean that their boss would not kill them for failing.

I found that Jessica had my duffle bag and my computer with her in the car. Every member of the Organization had a bag near the door, packed with everything they needed to just grab the bag and walk away from their home. It looked like I wasn't going back to my little apartment. I pulled out my mp3 player and listened to some loud music as I watched the street lights blur. I was fighting exhaustion.

Jessica was silent most of the way to the Local Command Center. We finally pulled up to a private bank somewhere in a small city. I grabbed my bags and followed Jessica in a back door. We walked to a service elevator, when she ran an ID card through a scanner. The doors opened and we stepped inside. The elevator went down past what must be the vault and through another complex hidden several stories under the bank. I understood why this was a good hiding place for a command center; a private bank was a good cover for a lot of security and had a reason for being so deep underground. People could come and go at any time and seem like either customers or workers at the 24-hour bank. A bank also has a reason for requiring a lot of computers and hardware.

Without ever setting foot in the underground compound, I knew the layout and floor plan. Every Local Command Center was basically the same. I have been to the one in London and lived in the one in Moscow for a while. They all had a few things in common: each one had an Intelligence and head of Operations Center (IOC), training room, kitchen, recreational room, dorm rooms, small medical center, and so on. I still didn't know every room in the complex, because there were a few things off-limits to me; mostly because I was not a full member. I wasn't allowed in the IOC or the armory, but that did not really bother me. I always had something to do and kept busy.

Jessica walked up to a man I recognized instantly. First, he stands out in most groups, and secondly, I have been training with him every day for the last three years or so.

"Here she is, Nick. I have to go, I'll be missed if I stay any longer." With that, Jessica turned and left the way we came.

"Are you alright?" he asked me in a quiet and tired voice.

"Yeah, I'm fine," I answered.

"Matt just arrived, you can see him after you write up what happened." Nick pointed to a table with papers waiting.

"Paperwork! Really? I was almost kidnapped and you want me to do paperwork?" I asked incredulously.

"Holly, you know the rules. When something like this happens, you write it up, and it gets filed away. Arguing with me won't change that. I don't make the rules," he stole the argument right out of my mouth.

I sat down and recorded what happened that day. When I had finished, I looked at Nick with my eyebrows raised, silently asking if I was allowed to go. He crossed his arms and nodded, then mumbled under his breath, "What am I going to do with you?"

I hurried off to find Matt. It wasn't hard. Like a typical teenage guy, he was in the kitchen. He was sitting on the countertop eating chips. He looked up as I walked in.

"Holly! You're here! What happened to you? I heard you were kidnapped right after we said good-bye," concern was all over his face.

I sat next to him on the counter and helped myself to his chips. "Yup, I was grabbed and woke up in the trunk of some car. I fought my way out and found out they were supposed to grab you, too."

"Yeah, yeah, I heard that, but what happened after that?" he asked impatiently.

"I called their boss and made one of them talk to him and made a deal to meet in three days in the parking garage of a casino. Then I hung up and knocked the two guys out, but I wouldn't kill them. I made it look like they were in a car crash. They can't tell the cops how they really got the injuries. 'Well Mr. Policeman, I kidnapped a girl and she beat us up', you know what I mean? Plus, we can follow them to wherever they go and find out who else is in on it."

"Holly, that's genius!" he smiled at me.

"All because I refuse to kill some thugs," I mumbled leaning my head against the cupboard, sighing and closing my eyes. I found I was more tired than I had thought.

"I'll make you a deal. If you answer me one question, I'll tell you where your room is," he offered.

"What do you want to know?" I asked.

"What's your last name?" he asked quietly.

"Matt, we have been over this. I can't tell you and you can't tell me, it's the rules. It keeps us safe," I told him. I knew he didn't mean any harm by it, but I couldn't tell.

"You've broken the rules before," he replied.

"I have bent them or found loopholes, but have not broken the rules. Either way, I made a promise and those, I don't break," I said with my eyes closed.

"Don't you want to know where your room is?" he asked, baiting me.

I hopped off the counter and told him, "No, I will find it myself." With that, I walked out and off to find an empty room.

"Wait Holly, come back. I'm sorry. I didn't mean it!" he called after me. I ignored his apology and kept looking for the right door.

I found the dorms easily and started searching for my room. Most of them were locked, but one on the end was open and my bags were sitting on the bed. I set the bags on the floor and flopped onto the bed. A wave of fatigue swept over me and I fell asleep almost instantly. As I slept, I started to dream.

Chapter 2

I heard the breaking of glass and something heavy hit the hardwood floor. I sat up and looked around. The room was small, cramped. It was full of toys and other toddler things, things I haven't seen in ten years. The clock on the bedside table read 3:00 AM. I threw off the covers and looked in the mirror hanging on the wall. I was six again, in our old apartment in Moscow, Russia.

I never called it home; I moved around too much to call anywhere home. But it was where my mother and I had lived back then. We moved from apartment to apartment every few months all across the world. I didn't know why - not back then anyway.

I walked to the door, opened it, and peeked into the hallway. I saw smoke and an orange glow flickering from the living room. My mother taught me what to do if there ever was a fire - get her. I ran to her room and knocked on the door. No response came. I called and pounded my tiny fists on the thin wooden door. It made no difference. The smoke was becoming thick. It stung my eyes and nose; I started to cough. I pulled on the door knob and found it locked. The hall was getting hotter. The smoke was filling my lungs and burning them, making me cough harder. I screamed, still nothing. I had once seen my mother break down a door to get to me when I slipped and hit my head in the bathroom. I put my shoulder to the door and pushed. The door held. I took a few steps back and slammed my shoulder into the door, achieving nothing but a sore shoulder. I just didn't understand why she would not wake up, why was she not helping me? I could hear sirens outside.

I heard the front door crash open and a dark figure sprinted towards me. I tried to scream, but was coughing too hard. I expected to see a fire fighter, but this man was wearing a black suit and sunglasses. This was pointless in my opinion, because it was 3:00 AM. He slammed his whole weight onto the door, and it easily gave way. He sprinted into my mother's room without stopping for a second. I tried to follow, but I couldn't catch my breath. I was holding myself up by clinging to the wall. He returned suddenly with the black duffle bag my mother took everywhere with her. He picked me up and hurried outside. I felt panicky, but I couldn't move. My vision slipped and my body felt numb. I blacked out from all the smoke.

I woke up in a hospital bed. I watched through a window as a woman I recognized signed papers and talked to nurses. All the time looking or pointing at me as they talked. After hours in the hospital, I was released into the care of Miss Cassidy. She was a friend of my mother who also came to watch me when my mother left for work or for days on end with no explanation. Silently, Miss Cassidy helped me into her car, and we drove without saying a word for hours.

The car pulled over, and we got out in an empty lot. I walked a few steps from the car, trying to figure out where we were. Another car pulled up, and Miss Cassidy greeted the driver. She transferred the bags into the new car and opened the door for me. I climbed into the backseat and she sat in the passenger seat. As we pulled onto the main road, I glanced back and saw the car we left in the lot burst into flames. I turned back around to look at Miss Cassidy for an explanation. She told me they had to get rid of the car so no one could follow us.

I woke up covered in a cold sweat. It had been years since I had relived my mother's death. I looked around the room. It was dark, but I was in the underground complex. I was safe. I threw the covers off and grabbed my bag, then walked quietly down the hall and into the bathroom to take a shower. The hot water rinsed away the nightmare, and I changed into a T-shirt and shorts. I wanted to run (free running was how I did my best thinking), but I wasn't cleared to leave the bank. From my room, I grabbed my mp3 player and towel, plus a water bottle from the kitchen. I decided to work out even if I couldn't go anywhere. I found a treadmill in the training room. I waved at the security camera to let the guys know I was fine. As I turned on the treadmill, I glanced at the clock on the wall, 2:26 AM. That was why the halls and kitchen were mostly deserted. Oh well, because of the six hour shift, there was always someone up and working. The cook even served four meals, one at 6:00 AM, noon, 6:00 PM, and midnight. The rest of the time you just grabbed what you needed. I put the headphones on, blasting music into my ears, and cranked the speed on the treadmill to seven. At first, I tried not to think at all. I did not want to remember her, my mother. Everyone has lost something and stewing in that horrific memory wouldn't do me any good, but it was a losing battle. Tears started to stream down as I remembered her face, her smile, the way she walked. I ran 'til I finished the playlist. I had run blindly for three hours. I turned off the treadmill and looked for something else to do. I drank some water, wiped my eyes, and started opening boxes and cabinets. I came across a set of throwing knives. I set up the target and threw the knives into a wooden mannequin. With the mp3 player blasting, I kept beat with the soft thud of the knife hitting the wood. As the beat got faster, so did the knives. My adrenaline pumped, and even with the music, I could hear the vent and soft hum of the lights. The music screamed into my ears, and the knives hit harder and harder. Suddenly, I heard a bang behind me. I turned towards the sound, hurling my last knife.

I stared into the face of Dimitri, who stared coolly back with a knife lodged in the wall just over his head.

"I thought that brother of mine had taught you better. You know it's rude to throw knives at people's faces," he said with one eyebrow raised. He looked just like his twin Nick, other than a few differences: Dimitri has a small scar over his left eye and shorter hair. But personality wise, they were night and day. Nick was responsible, even-tempered, reasonable, loyal, strict, and professional. Whereas his brother was more carefree, capricious, headstrong, and fun-loving. Other than looks, they had one big thing in common - they were both very good at their job. They also both had decided to specialize in training rather than pursuing higher ranks as agents.

"Sorry, I…you surprised me." I apologized quietly while pulling my headphones out.

"Nightmares again?" he asked, looking at my puffy red eyes.

"No," I lied, not looking at him.

"Of your mother?" he pressed.

"No," I repeated more firmly, still not looking at him.

"No, as in, 'no, not her', or 'no, you're not having nightmares'?"

"As in, 'no, I don't want to talk about it'," I said as I turned to pull the knives from the target.

"Fine, but you still can't lie very well. I thought you were getting good when I started to teach you poker. Maybe it's just the subject." He leaned against the wall and crossed his arms. "You know you look just like her," he added as an afterthought.

"What do you know?" I said putting the knives away.

"I know she would be proud of you," he said quietly.

"You never met her," I retorted.

"No, you're right, but I'm proud of you," he said as I finally meet his gaze.

"Do you want something Dimitri, or did you just want to chat?" I asked sarcastically.

"I propose a trade of the most valuable thing in this business: information. You give me the local gossip; and I give you the international info, and what I just heard from the head of local operations," he offered.

"Alright, I just got kidnapped and escaped. They were after Matt and me so we will be hanging here 'til somebody decides what to do with us. I also set up a meeting with the guy who paid the kidnappers in the casino's parking garage."

"Are you alright?" he asked, more seriously.

"I'm fine, now your turn!" I sat on a bench nearby and wiped my face and neck with a hand towel, waiting for him to start.

"Leah is back in the states from Africa. Wren, Eagle, and Falcon are being deployed, but no one seems to know where or for what. Hawk is dead, his cover was blown in North Korea. Kodiak is missing, he disappeared in Iran. They have someone looking for him, but it's probably too late. Grizzly is all bent up over it, so they gave him a month's leave to see his family. Lucky guy, I haven't seen Chloe in six months." He trailed off and sat next to me on the bench.

"How old is she now?" I asked.

"She is six now, I just missed her birthday party. We talk all the time, over the phone and with a web cam. It broke my heart when she asked when I'm coming home. Linda sent me a picture." He pulled a small bent picture out of his wallet. It showed a small girl, smiling at the camera, dressed in a pink dress and tiara. She was surrounded by other small, smiling faces as Chloe ripped open presents.

"So you talked to the Head of Local Operations," I prompted, trying to stay on topic. We could talk about Chloe later.

"Yup, I talked to him, he said he wants to see you at 0700. The secretary will let you in. So get cleaned up and have some breakfast. Good luck, kid." He patted my shoulder and started towards the door.

I groaned and buried my face in my hands. It's never a good thing, when the local boss wants to see you. Unless we were in trouble, they mostly left the trainees alone. I looked at myself in the mirror. I was a sweaty mess. I followed Dimitri out of the gym and went up to take my second shower of the day. I had a sneaking suspicion that it wasn't going to be my last.

After the shower I changed into jeans, a T-shirt, and my favorite leather jacket, taking a minute to grab my phone and knife, which I try to always have on me. I made my way into the kitchen and dug around 'til I found a bagel and some cream cheese to smear on it. I poured some orange juice and grabbed a banana as well. The dining room was mostly empty, so I sat next to Nick and started eating.

"Dimitri said you were up and had started to work out," he said as he sipped black coffee.

"Couldn't sleep," I replied with a shrug.

"Local Head of Operations wants to see you," he told me without looking up.

"Yeah, I heard," I glared at my food and continued eating.

"Do you know when?" he asked, looking at a large clock on the wall.

"Dimitri said at 7," I replied finishing off my bagel.

"That would be in 4 minutes," he said in a quiet matter-of-fact voice.

"Oh, crap!" I had to be on time for that. I started to gather all my food up.

"I'll get that, you should get going," he said and continued to eat.

"Thanks," I called over my shoulder as I sprinted out of the dining room and up to the Intelligence and Head of Operations Center. I stopped at the heavy reinforced metal door and looked at the clock on my cell phone, 7:00 AM exactly. I heard a small beep and the door swung easily on its hinges to reveal a thin red-headed woman of about twenty five. She was dressed in a black skirt and a too-tight purple blouse as well as black high heels.

"Follow me, and don't touch anything", she said as she looked down her nose at me, like I was going to infect her with something. I already didn't like her. She turned and disappeared inside the IOC. I followed close behind as the door slammed shut behind me.

The room was immense and filled with cubicles and desks. People talked on headsets or on webcams. Others dashed in and out of cubicles or offices carrying papers or files and things of that nature. Massive TV screens flashed due dates, deadlines, names, places, and requests. It was an overwhelming hive of activity. The red-headed secretary was hurrying off through the cubicles with me trailing in her wake. She stopped at a door marked *Director* and knocked.

"Come in," came a deep raspy voice from within. The secretary opened the door, rudely pushed me in, and closed the door again. The office was furnished in dark wood, had thick red carpeting, and reeked of cigar smoke. Lining one wall was a bookshelf filled with leather-bound books and small glass cases holding a variety of guns or medals from some war. Seated behind the large desk was a portly, balding man in a tailored suit. He was puffing on a fat cigar, creating a slight haze in the office. He motioned for me to sit in the uncomfortable wooden chair in front of the desk. I perched myself on the hard straight-backed chair feeling very much like a misbehaved child in the principal's office.

"It has come to my attention that you and Matt have been discovered. Have you done anything in the last month or so that could compromise your anonymity?" he asked impersonally and businesslike as he took another pull from his cigar.

"No, we never speak or hang out in public. We never enter or leave a building at the same time. I have never contacted him though the internet or over unsecure lines," I said, thinking back over the last few weeks.

"What about training?" he asked, looking at the file on his desk.

"Matt and I have always followed the path set out by Tonya to meet up with Nick, avoiding cameras and people. It was always by the book. I may not like all of the rules, but I followed them to the letter. "

"Not even after training?" he asked, probing.

I shifted in my seat, "Sometimes we talked on the roof, but we climbed up one at a time and left that way, too," I admitted.

"I see," he wrote something down on a paper in the file. "And that is it?" he asked.

"Yes, sir," I responded automatically.

"Well, I think that covers that situation. I want to talk about how you handled your abduction," he said, tapping some ash into a tray and placing the cigar back in his mouth. "You showed unexpected bravery, quick thinking, and very creative problem solving. Making it look like a car crash, where did you learn that?" he inquired. But not waiting for me to answer, he launched on. "That said, I am still in favor of throwing you out into the streets or putting you in foster care. You broke the first and biggest rule: never disobey an order. Just because your mother was one of our best does not mean you get special treatment. You have been with this organization for almost ten years and you still can't get that. Are you stupid or just arrogant?" his voice was steadily getting louder, "You think you're better that the rest of us, that you alone know what is best, despite the fact that Tonya and the rest of the handlers have access to information and resources you can't even begin to dream of!" I shrank back into the chair, not daring to answer or try to defend myself. His expression softened and he settled back in his leather chair and took another puff on his cigar. He continued calmly and quietly, "However, the decision is not mine to make. The situation has attracted the attention of other Directors. They are giving you a chance to redeem yourself. You will be allowed to participate in your first mission, in fact, you will be playing a key part in the operation in the casino parking garage. In the meantime, you are not to leave the complex and you need to hand over your cell phone."

I stared at him in shocked disbelief. I had never done anything big for the Organization. If anything, I was sent on stakeouts and guard duty. My main job was to learn; to excel in math, history, languages, marksmanship, martial arts, emergency medical aid, weapons knowledge, interrogating, counter-interrogation, and anything else Nick trained me in. Compared to the other jobs in the Organization, my job was easy.

"Will you do it?" he asked, clearly enjoying the impression he had made.

"Yes," it was all I could say. You never refuse a job, not if you wanted to stay with the Organization. I handed him my cell phone.

"Alright then, don't mess this one up," he warned as he took my phone. He was not particularly encouraging. "You had better get off to the gym, your training with Matt started 25 minutes ago." He dismissed me as he glanced at his watch.

I got up and left the office. The rude secretary was waiting for me and, without a word, she turned and led me back to the door. She punched in a code and slid a card through a scanner. The door swung soundlessly on its hinges to let me out. I hurried down the hall and back to my room, quickly changing into basketball shorts and a tank top. I found Matt, Nick and Barracuda with his trainee, Emily. Most trainees are paired up and later go on to work as a team, but a few are trained individually. Not everyone has the personality for constant teamwork. Emily certainly didn't. Matt and Emily sparred as I warmed up and stretched. Nick and Barracuda gave Matt tips on fighting but it hardly made a difference, Emily was older and more experienced. She was so graceful and fast, making him look clumsy and sluggish. Barracuda called it off after she pinned Matt for the fifth time.

"Don't feel bad Matt, I taught her all she knows. No one her age can beat Emily," Barracuda boasted in his deep, slow voice. He was taller than Nick and built like a linebacker. His bare arms bulged with muscles and were covered in tattoos.

"Holly has been training since she was 6, if anyone can beat Emily, it's her," Nick replied in a cool tone with raised eyebrows, looking at Barracuda.

I internally rolled my eyes. Trainees were always a source of pride for trainers, like parents bragging about their kids. Friendly competition and rivalry was common between the trainers, often spilling over to the kids.

"How about it, Holly? Want to see if you can beat me?" Emily challenged as she gave me a cocky smile and put her hands on her hips. Over her shoulder, Nick was looking expectantly at me. Matt was rubbing his bruises. There was no way for me to back down with my dignity intact.

"Sure, why not," I shrugged, trying to look like I hardly cared. I stepped onto the mat.

All operatives are taught the same combination of martial arts;

however, a trainer's style has a huge influence on their trainee's style. The rules of a sparring match are simple: no killing, no maiming, no outside interference, keep it on the mat, and stop when your opponent is pinned to the mat.

We circled each other for a second. I stepped in, faking a blow to her face, and she blocked, leaving her side open. I punched her in the ribs and stepped back out of range. She turned and kicked at my chest. I caught it and lifted it over my head, and quickly swept her other leg out from under her. Emily crumpled to the mat landing on her back. Shock was evident on her face, but it hastily turned to determination. I crouched and caught her foot under my arm. She kicked her other leg at my head and I blocked it with my arm. I could tell she was pissed now, Emily was not accustomed to losing. She ripped her foot from me and kicked my stomach, nearly knocking the air out of me. I stumbled back, but stayed on my feet. Emily sprang to her feet. We circled each other again. The room was filling up with spectators watching the fight. The pressure was on, but we were trained to excel under pressure and extreme circumstances. I swept at her feet, but she jumped. She punched at my face. I caught it, twisted her arm into an arm bar, and drove her face first into the mat. Emily hit the mat with a slap, and I heard her teeth knock together. She let out a soft moan. I heard cheers from one half of the room. I pinned her loose hand under mine. She reversed my hold on her wrists and trapped mine instead. Emily curled into a ball on her side and kicked me in the chest, hard. I fell back landing on my butt. My ribs ached, but they weren't broken. Emily launched herself on top of me. The other half of the room let out a cheer. I tried to roll away, but she wrapped her arm around my neck. Emily had me in a head lock. I pushed up on her elbow and turned my head in. She pinned my legs under her own.

"I read a file on your mother," Emily whispered into my ear as I tried to pull her off me. "It said you're a bastard; no one knows who your father is." I bucked my head into her chin, but not hard enough to do me any good. "Your mother was a whore and a slut," she continued viciously. My focus was slipping, and I was seeing red. I was trained to fight through pain and distractions, but rage was another story. "How much do you think your daddy had to pay? It couldn't be too much, your mom wasn't *that* good looking." I slammed my fist into her face and felt a satisfying crunch of her nose breaking. "Bitch," she spat at me through the blood pouring down her face. She rolled me over and pinned me to the mat. Emily tightened her chokehold. Black spots popped in front of my eyes, and I started to shake as I gasped for air.

"Enough!" shouted Dimitri. I felt Emily's weight lift off me, and she let me out of the chokehold. Air rushed back into my lungs, and the room stopped spinning. A hand grabbed my upper arm and pulled me to my feet. I looked up into Nick's face as he steadied me. His face was an odd mix of concern and disappointment. I glanced about the room and saw it crowded with people standing around a bloody mat, still watching me.

"Matt, take Emily and Holly to the infirmary," ordered Dimitri.

"No, we can walk, sir," I pulled Nick's hand from my arm and walked out the door. The adrenaline in my veins faded away, leaving me feeling humiliated, sore, and livid at Emily.

We walked down the hall towards the infirmary. I looked up and down the hall for people and cameras, finding it void of both. Emily was a few paces behind me cupping her hands around her nose, glaring at the floor. Making a snap decision, I turned and punched her in the face, her head snapped back, and she fell to the ground. Emily let out a small gasp of shock and pain.

"Shit, Holly, that was a cheap shot," she said, holding the side of her face, but not getting up or fighting back.

"So was talking crap about my mom," I glared down at her huddled form.

"Look, it wasn't personal, I just had to win. Barracuda said if I lost to you, he would-" She tried to explain, but I cut her off.

"It doesn't get more personal than calling someone's mom a whore," I replied.

"I'm not here to make friends, I'm here to be the best and start a career. Sometimes that means stepping on a few people. If you really are as good as everyone says you are, you would have been able to fight through trash talking," she said pulling herself up to her feet.

I gave her a look of loathing and disgust, turning my back on her I walked off to the infirmary to get patched up.

Chapter 3

I walked into the dining room holding an ice pack to my throbbing, taped up ribs. It was mostly empty. I had just missed dinner, since I was in the infirmary trying to convince the doctors that I did not have a concussion and listening to the unpleasant sounds of Emily's nose being reset. Walking through the room, I spotted Ryan sitting alone with an untouched plate sitting next to him and files spread out all over the table. He was a trainee too, but a different kind. Ryan worked as a handler's assistant and hacker. We met through a few mock operations, and he had just transferred from London a few weeks ago. Ryan was small, thin, and was so pale he looked like he hadn't seen the sun in months. I slid into the chair next to him and looked over his shoulder at the papers everywhere. He didn't notice me.

"Good read?"I asked him. Ryan jumped like he had been electrocuted.

"Bloody hell, don't do that to me," he yelped. He recovered some and looked at me more closely. "God, Holly, what happened to you?"

"Sparring," I explained simply.

"With a brick wall?" he asked, eyeing my ice pack.

"No, with Emily," I told him as I started to eat off his now cold plate. He didn't mind or really notice.

"You know, the problem with this place is you don't see any real cat fights. There's no screaming, scratching, hair pulling, or name calling. Just blood, broken bones, and such. Not as much fun," he said shaking his head in mock despair.

"Ryan, you really need a girlfriend," I told him as I continued to eat.

"Is that an offer?" he asked hopefully.

"You wish," I rolled my eyes.

"I'll try again later then, shall I?" he said grinning.

"I'd rather you didn't," I replied in between bites of mashed potatoes.

"So tell me what happened, it must have been a good fight if you're this hurt" he asked, thankfully changing the subject. I recounted the match blow by blow, but I hesitated when I came to the part about what Emily had said to me.

"You can trust me, love. I don't sell what you tell me, ever," he prompted.

I studied his face for a second, then told him everything.

"That lying bitch!" he cried in outrage at what Emily had said.

"I know, but the part the worries me is how she read a file on ... hang on, how do you know she was lying?" I asked him with a raised eyebrow.

"Some of the blokes back home told unbelievable stories 'bout your mum to us trainees and I had an, let's call it an 'opportunity', to read 'er file," Ryan shifted uncomfortably in his chair. "It was all legend, you know, made up stuff about 'er- and none of it said she has an illegitimate daughter. It just said she had a kid that went into the Organization after she died. So either the real file is hidden somewhere else, or it was deleted. One way or another, your mum was neck deep in some serious clandestine stuff and Emily is making stuff up 'bout it to piss you off."

I opened my mouth to tell Ryan what I thought about him snooping through my mom's files, then Matt came running into the dining room.

"Holly, there you are! Hurry up or you're going to miss out on the fun," he told me excitedly.

"What fun? Is someone else pounding Emily's face in?" I said almost hopefully.

"Wait, you gave her the black eye?" he asked confused.

"No, of course I didn't," I said as I nodded my head yes, conveying that I did punch Emily, but not to spread it around.

"I think Emily is still in the infirmary." Matt gave me an unsure look then switched back to what he came to tell me. "The operatives cleared a conference room and are setting up a game of soccer, hurry up or you will be sitting on the sidelines." Matt turned to lead the way, and I stood to follow. Ryan shoved the papers on the table into a manila file folder and stood too. Noticing this Matt told Ryan, "It's an operative-only game, besides you wouldn't be able to keep up."

"That's real subtle, that is," Ryan replied sarcastically. "I'm off to turn in my assignment, not crash your little game." With that he left the room heading to the IOC.

"I don't trust him," Matt said more to himself than to me, staring after Ryan. All traces of his excitement now where gone. With that he turned and walked down the hall towards the conference rooms. I followed. I had been up since 3:00, my ribs hurt and so did my pride, but the game was likely the only recreation I was going to get all day.

"Did the Director talk to you by any chance?" I asked looking sideways at Matt.

"Yeah, why?" he asked me.

"Because he talked to me too, said I'm working in the casino operation," I informed him.

"Same here. Any idea how they're going to play this one out?" he asked.

"I can guess. I think we're going to be bait. The guy that paid the kidnapers must have a reason for targeting us, and if it has any connection to the Organization the Directors are going to be very interested in what that reason is...." I trailed off, lost in thought.

"Well, if you and I are going to be bait, it's not smart to stay mad at each other. So, sorry about last night," he apologized.

"You're forgiven, but don't ask again. Some information is not meant to be shared," I told him.

"Deal, now let's hurry. I don't want to be picked last." Matt broke into a run with me on his heels.

The game of soccer turned out to be more fun than I'd had in weeks, maybe even months. The conference room was large enough to resemble a small football field. The tables and chairs were pushed to the sides and whiteboards served as goals. Duct tape was laid on the floor to show the boundary lines. The twins were our self-appointed captains and proved to be extremely competitive. I was on Nick's team and Matt was on Dimitri's. Emily sat on the sidelines, holding an ice pack to her face. I could see that her nose was taped up. One of Emily's eyes was swollen shut as it turned black and blue. She half-heartedly cheered on Barracuda who was on Dimitri's team. The game lasted 2 hours, and because there was no real referee, few people followed rules or kept score fairly. This inevitably lead to arguments and fights. In the end, my team won 6 to 4, or at least we think is was 6 to 4.

After the game, everyone helped put the room back together and clean up. Once finished I went to take my 3rd and final shower of the day. I pulled on my pajamas and brushed my teeth as I glanced in the mirror. The cuts and scrapes from my kidnapping were scabbing over. My ribs still throbbed and ached. Across my throat was a dark bruise from Emily's choke hold. I fingered it gingerly and winced. Well, at least I didn't have a black eye or broken nose. I dragged myself down the hall and into my room. I turned the lights off and curled up under the covers. One of the nice things about working for the Organization was that insomnia was never a problem. After a few minutes in the pitch black, silent, underground room, I was out. I started to drift and dream.

I was standing in a dirty, snow-covered alleyway surrounded by seven kids my age and older. We all wore heavy winter boots, ill-fitting coats, tattered scarves, dirty gloves, and knit hats. I was in a small rundown town in Russia near the "boarding school" or Training Command Center. The TCC was ironically housed under a real boarding school. In the afternoon, the kids were sent outside to play, but ended up dividing into gangs which were headed by the elder students. The ragtag children caused mayhem in the small town by pick-pocketing, stealing unattended cars and leaving them on the other side of town, looting stores for candy, breaking into houses for fun, and having mini harmless gang wars. The wars mostly involved a lot of screaming, swearing, spray-painting and rock throwing. And I loved every second of it. I was better at it than most of the other 9 year olds. Rocky, I'm sure that wasn't his real name, noticed this and worked me harder than the others, trying to improve my knack and turn it into something more.

On that particular day, the gang I was in was setting up to break into a small house. Rocky had named us the Shadow Bandits. He was not all that imaginative. Most of the kids were a blur to me. I couldn't remember their names or faces, but I can remember Rocky and a little girl named Sophie, perfectly. As we younger kids shifted from one foot to the other in the biting cold, Rocky stood on a trash can and gave orders. Sophie was holding my hand, watching everything with her huge, brown, doe eyes.

Our mark was a house in the residential area owned by a bank teller. We knew he worked the evening shift. He also took the bus to and from work, giving us opportunity. Rocky gave everyone their instructions, and we filed out of the alley and through the neighborhood. It was about 1:00 pm and our mark would be waiting for the bus down the street about now. I broke off from the group and walked to the bus stop. The rest of the Shadow Bandits continued to wait near the mark's house.

I shuffled my feet when I approached the bus stop and stared at the ground as I walked along. The man was standing facing the street holding a briefcase. I could see both his wallet and his keys were in his right pocket. I walked next to him and bumped into him hard and fell to the ground. The mark turned around and helped me to my feet. I apologized and walked on my way with his keys in my coat pocket.

When I arrived at the mark's house, the gang was waiting on the porch. I opened the door, and we all filed in and spread out, each kid searching one room. I had the bedroom. I looked in the dresser, under the bed, and rooted around in the closet, finding nothing of interest. I pulled open the drawer in the bedside table and found a beautiful silver chunk of metal. I picked it up, and I pressed the small button on the side. A thin razor-sharp blade popped out of the end. I stared in amazement at the little knife. It was a switchblade. I had seen them before but never held one. Certainly not one like this. The switchblades I had seen were beat up and handed down, usually with a wooden handle. This one was pristine, polished, and had something engraved in the handle. I retracted the blade and slipped it into my pocket. I was told to bring everything I found to Rocky, but I decided to keep the little knife. I poked around and found a little wad of cash in the drawer and decided to give that to Rocky instead. Everyone met up at the front door and handed over their finds to our boss. Rocky tucked all the loot into his pockets and we left. I locked the door and dropped the keys on the sidewalk so the mark would think he had dropped them walking to the bus.

We were almost out of the neighborhood, when a rival gang cut us off. They were a smaller gang, only 5 members, but they were older. They asked us what we were doing in their territory and told us to hand over any loot we had just taken. We refused and started off in another direction. They cut us off again and bragged about *stealing from the arms store. The leader pulled out a small handgun and pointed it at Rocky and told him to hand over the loot. A boy in our gang picked up a stone and threw it at their leader. His aim was impressive and it struck the armed leader in the eye. He fell back and the muzzle flashed. Everyone stood perfectly still for a second in shock. Someone screamed and we all ran for it. I turned to find Sophie to make sure she was with me. She was lying on the pavement, face up, her doe eyes wide in shock. She had a small round hole in her forehead. Blood trickled from the hole and the corner of her mouth.*

I shot up in my bed. I looked around and realized were I was. I was clutching the sheets and had to force myself to let go. Tears were running down my face. I was shaking and covered in a cold sweat. I picked up my switchblade off the bedside table. I traced my finger over the engraved silver handle. My door flew open causing me to jump and squint into the light.

"Holly? Are you ok?" It was Matt. He stepped into the room and I saw his face. He was clearly worried.

"Um...yeah I'm fine," I reassured him, while I tried to get my breathing and heart rate down.

"No you're not, what's the matter," he wasn't buying it. "You're crying, you almost never cry."

"I'm fine really, it was just a bad dream," I told him.

He shifted his weight back and forth, he was reluctant to go. "Want to tell me about it?"

"No," I said simply.

"I could stay if you want," he offered.

I looked over at the clock, it was 4 am. "No thanks, you should go back to bed. It's late."

" I don't care, I don't mind staying up," he told me.

I groaned and pulled the covers over my head. "Good night, Matt," I said pointedly. He lingered for a minute then closed the door. I fell back asleep and, thankfully, slept without dreaming.

I woke up at 6:30 and took a quick shower, dressed and went to the dining room for breakfast. The dining room was full and the smell of bacon, eggs, biscuits and sausage made my stomach growl. I filled my plate and found a spot next to Nick. After breakfast, everyone filed into the briefing room and the plan for the mission was laid out.

Two hours before dark, six black cars and one service van pulled out of the bank's parking lot and took separate routes to the casino. Once there, the cars spread out through the bottom level of the garage. Matt and I were left standing in the center under a florescent light.

Our hands were secured behind our backs with handcuffs that would pop open if you put enough torque on them. We were wearing small Kevlar vests covered by baggy sweatshirts in case things went bad.

The service van pulled up next to us and the door opened to reveal Markus, my kidnapper. He had a leg brace on and looked unhappy to be there. He was pushed out and limped near us. He was told that if he did not do exactly as he was told, he would be shot by a sniper at the other end of the parking garage. The van disappeared and all of the operatives seemed to melt into the walls, leaving Markus, Matt, and I seemingly alone in the center of the garage. It was so silent my every breath sounded like thunder in my ears. I was nervous and had adrenaline rippling through my veins. I jumped a little, when two black SUVs tore in and pulled up across from us. Four men in suits and balaclavas stepped out, but stood about 8 feet back. Two stood in front of the others holding submachine guns, one stood holding a black duffle bag, and the remaining man was evidently the boss. His suit was designer, and his body language screamed "I'm in charge".

"What happened to you?" asked the leader.

"You didn't tell me they could fight." Markus replied with a glare.

"Where is the other guy? Wasn't there two of you?" asked one of the men with a submachine gun.

"He is in the hospital, thanks to this one." He grabbed me by the hair and pulled it back so my face was to the ceiling. I saw a glint in his eye. He wanted to get revenge for what I did to him and his friend, but knew he couldn't. I was in his hands, and he could do nothing about it. It would have been easy to break a bone in the idiot's arm, but I refrained. "So do I get paid or what?" Markus asked impatiently. Unknown to the four men, Markus was anxious to have the sniper off his back. The man carrying the black duffle bag stepped forward. He threw it to Markus, who shoved me and Matt over to the men.

"They seem rather lethargic and docile," pointed out the leader.

"I drugged them, it will wear off in a few hours," Markus informed them and heaved the bag over his shoulder. He turned to leave.

"Markus," the boss called as Markus walked away. "You forgot to give us the key to the cuffs." Markus turned back and tossed the key to them. Then, with his money, he slipped from view between cars.

The men clamped a second set of cuffs on us and used the key to unlock the first and tossed them in a trash can nearby. So much for our rigged cuffs. One guy checked our jean pockets, but found nothing. While they did this an Operative crawled up to the SUVs and stuck a tracking device on the undercarriage. The men didn't notice and went on to pull black cloth hoods over our heads, rendering us blind. I felt myself being shoved into the car and heard the door slam.

The car lurched forward, and I heard the tires squeal. Matt wasn't in the car with me so he must have been in the other car. The ride was silent and stretched on for hours. Eventually, the car stopped and I was hauled out, pushed up a few stairs, and sat in a canvas seat. Rough hands strapped me in. A deafening motor sound started up, and we moved forward. We moved faster and faster until, I felt the familiar feeling of G forces pushing me deeper into the seat. Suddenly, the pieces fell together. I was on a plane; it was loud and small so it had to be a private plane. I heard Matt breathing next to me.

"Matt, are you okay?" I whispered.

"Yeah, you?" he asked just as quietly.

"I'm fine. Where could we be flying to?" I inquired.

"No idea," he replied.

"Hey, shut it over there!" one of the men called. Matt and I promptly ceased our conversation. After a boring 3 hours, I was unbuckled and pulled out of my seat. I stumbled down the walkway with a hand in the small of my back prodding me on. A door was pulled open, and I was pushed in. The hood was whipped off, and I squinted in the light. I was in the bathroom of a plane.

"Take care of business. Hurry and don't try anything," warned the man with the submachine gun. He patted the gun for emphasis. His face was still hidden by the mask.

"That's going to be interesting with these on," I pointed out holding up my handcuffs.

"You'll manage," he said with a smirk. He shut the door and locked it.

I grabbed my phone that was tucked into my sock and looked at the text on it. Thank God they didn't search me or Matt. The text was from Tonya: *We have a fix on your location, you're heading to Hawaii. Stay safe.* I put my phone back in my pocket and cleaned up. The door opened and my hood was replaced. I was guided back to my seat and strapped in. Matt was taken next and returned after a few minutes.

"You know we're heading to Hawaii?" Matt asked under his breath.

"I got that text, too," I replied. I tried to role my shoulders to make my equipment lie flat and stop poking me in the back, but sadly I had no success.

"I've always wanted to go," he said trying to make the best of what we have.

"I told you to shut up!" shouted one of the men. "Next one to whisper takes a dive out of the plane, without a parachute," he threatened. We decided not to take him up on the offer.

The plane flew on for about 3 hours. I tried to sleep but nerves and worry kept me up. After what must have been about 6 hours, the plane landed and Matt and I went for another car ride.

This ride was significantly shorter, and we were dragged out of the car. I was marched into an air-conditioned building up a long flight of stairs. I heard the metallic rattling of an old furnace. I counted my steps as I went along, making a mental floor plan. Matt and I were separated. I was pushed into a room and sat on a hard metal chair with my hands chained in front of me to a table. The room was bright and tiny pinpricks of light penetrated the hood which was quickly yanked off. I took stock of my surroundings.

The room was small with white walls, a large one-way mirror spanning most of one wall and one reinforced door. The metal table I was chained to was in the center of the room. I sat on one side, a woman sat on the other. A guard was posted at the door with a submachine gun. I looked the gun over and noted something that almost made me laugh. I kept the detail to myself. The woman was Asian and dressed in a feminine business suit with a plunging neckline. The guard could hardly stop staring at her. She was beautiful and she knew it. The woman had a clipboard in her lap tipped upwards so I couldn't see what it said.

"What is your name?" she asked, not looking up from the clipboard.

"You already know my name," I told her.

"What do you mean?" she asked sounding confused, but not very convincing.

"My kidnapper knew my name, and I highly doubt it was from his own research," I informed her.

"And why is that?" she asked with arched eyebrow clearly amused.

"He sucks as a kidnapper. I saw his papers on us when he moved me into a warehouse. Plus, it was easy enough to beat him up and put his friend in the hospital too. He was not very professional and likely got the information on who to take from whoever was paying him. My guess is that's you or at least your boss," I enlightened her, sounding bored. A small flash in her eyes told me I was right. Her posture changed, she was going on the defensive.

"That's an interesting theory," she spoke condescendingly. That annoyed me, but I didn't show it.

" I have another, but ask your questions and let's see if I'm right," I said.

She looked at my hair and wrote on the clipboard, then looked at my eyes and wrote something down.

"How tall are you?" she asked.

"Nine foot four" I lied pulling the number out of the air. She shot me a look that told me she did not appreciate me lying.

"Where were you born? How old are you?" she asked.

"It's not nice to ask a woman her age. So how old are you, sir?" I said. I was starting to get to her.

"You're not helping yourself. You're just making it worse, you know," she advised me. She stood up to make the next statement, looking me dead in the eye. She was livid and glared at me. "You have no idea what I can do to you," she threatened. The threat was empty. Her eyes shifted to the left just slightly at the end of the statement. Her brow knitted together in frustration. I decided to hit her where it would hurt, her looks.

"You might want to shave that mustache, it's not very attractive." She put a hand to her lip, but found nothing. She was losing her patience. The guard snickered, and the woman threw him a dirty look. She nodded pointedly at me to the guard who walked over and brushed my hair over my shoulder exposing the back of my neck. He shook his head at the woman.

My theory was right.

Chapter 4

The poor woman decided she'd had enough of my insolence. The hood was replaced over my face and my hands were cuffed behind me. I was pulled out of the room and lead down what must have been a hall. Again I counted my steps adding to my mental map. I heard another reinforced door open and I was dragged in the room. It was darker than the hallway, no pinpricks of light penetrated the hood this time. The guard pushed me to the ground and chained my cuffs to a metal loop in the concrete floor. I heard the door slam and knew he was gone. Judging by the silence in the room I was alone.

"Sound off," called someone in the room making me jump. Apparently I was mistaken.

"93315652," a girl called out her ID number; she sounded teenage but had an accent that I couldn't place.

"97896821," called out a boy; he had the same accent as the girl before. He sounded closer and to my right.

"12463543," called a teen with a Russian accent; his voice came from across the room.

"87846231," called out a boy with a Hispanic accent; he must have been next to the Russian.

"96648361," said a girl with a Canadian accent.

"71716931," said a boy in a Brazilian accent.

"98343571," called out a voice somewhere to my left; I recognized it as Matt.

I called out my own ID number "93058182"; I did so mostly out of habit. I was conditioned to sound off quickly and without much thought. The first number of the ID number is essentially an area code. One is Asia, two is Europe, three is the Middle East, four is the north half of Africa, five is the south half of Africa, six is the Pacific Islands and Australia, seven is for South America, eight is Central America and Mexico and finally nine is for North America. I don't know for sure, but I think the last number was how many generations of your family had worked for the Organization. Almost everyone was first generation and almost everyone's number ended in a 1. Mine however ended in a two, and I was a second generation Operative.

"Welcome, ladies and gents, we have 2 newcomers," said the person who had spoken first.

"Where are we?" asked Matt.

"I'm Luke, this is the holding room," said the boy with the unfamiliar accent. "Fun isn't it?" he added sarcastically. "Problem is, we have no idea what our coordinates are or what they want with us."

"I can answer both," I told them. "We're in Hawaii. I don't know what island but we have backup on the way. I think I know what-" I was cut off by the boy with the Russian accent.

"Vhat do you mean backup?" he asked bewildered. "No vone is coming. Ve are on our own."

"Hardly." I quickly explained that there was a plan to get us all out safe and sound, but refrained from telling them that it was.

"So vhat's da plan?" asked the Russian kid impatiently.

"What boarding school did you go to? Why on earth would I tell you what the plan is here, none of us can see what's in the room. For all we know, there is a bug or even another person. But we have backup coming. Keep on your toes and follow Matt's and my lead. Everyone will get out of this in one piece," I told them. I sat on my foot so my shoe reached my cuffed hands. I pulled off my shoe.

"But why take us in the first place?" asked Luke.

"Like I was trying to tell you, I know that too. They took note of my hair and eye color, asked me about my height and age. They wanted to know where I was born. When I pissed off the interrogator, she had my shoulder checked. They were looking for someone, a teen in the Organization. But they only know small details about the person. They also know that the person has a tattoo, scar, or birthmark on their neck. They know a basic description, but they don't know the gender of the teen. That's why they took both guys and girls. They also don't know where the operative is stationed, so they took teens from all over the world," I explained. I pulled a lock pick out of the sole of my shoe.

"So vhy can you tell us all zat, but not vhat da escape plan is?" asked the Russian.

"Because I don't care if they know that we know, what they do and don't know," I explained. I started to pick the lock of the chain binding my cuffs to the metal loop in the floor.

"What the hell is that supposed to mean," asked the girl with the same accent as Luke.

"She is testing whether or not they are listening to us," said Matt who was catching on.

"And I'm willing to bet that they are listening. I know the plan on breaking everyone out. If they have any intelligence at all, they will want to know what that is," I said as I freed my cuffs from the loop and switched my hands in front of me.

"So they take you, torture you, and you tell them everything. Then our people lose the element of surprise," said Luke; "great plan," he said sarcastically. His lack of confidence was annoying me.

"I really pissed off the interrogator. She won't want to talk with me again. So they'll bring out the big guns, her boss. Letting me see who's next up on the power chain. That will bring us closer to finding who paid for all this, and who they're looking for," I explained as I started to pick the cuffs.

"But if they are listening, they just heard the entire plan," pointed out the person who had spoken first.

"So they have to decide what's more important: knowing the escape plan and letting me walk all over the first interrogator and possibly getting more information out of her now that I know her tell. I saw the corners of her mouth tighten when she lies, or they could choose to let me see who outranks her by bringing in a higher ranking interrogator." I explained, then freed my hands of the cuffs, and pulled the hood off. The room was dark, I could hardly make out seven other kids, all of who were cuffed and wearing hoods like mine. There was nothing else in the room. Just us and a reinforced door. I crawled over to Matt and picked the lock on his handcuffs.

"But vhat if they just leave you here?" asked the Russian.

"Then they either can't hear us or think that they can fight off our backup without knowing the plan. The latter is the safer bet," I told them. I freed Matt, and he pulled a handcuff key out of his shoe and walked over to the kid next to him.

"Clever. Do you think that will really work?" asked the Canadian girl.

"I have no idea," I admitted simply. I pulled off the hood over the Canadian's head and held a finger up to my lips to silence her. The entire conversion had been to cover the noise of picking the locks and freeing the other kids.

Chapter 5

Matt and I freed the seven other trainees and huddled together in the corner to organize ourselves. Matt took off his sweatshirt and Kevlar vest. Under the vest, he had a Beretta M9 with a silencer taped across the back of his black t-shirt along with a combat knife, two head sets, and a flash bang. I unattached the equipment and handed it all to him then took off my sweatshirt and vest to do the same. I had the same equipment minus one headset. We split into three groups of three. Matt, the Canadian, and myself became team leaders and each took a linked headset. I quickly briefed the kids on the plan leaving a few key parts out. No one questioned the orders; we were trained not to ask too many questions.

"Ok, names would be helpful, I'm Holly, this is Matt," I explained. Matt nodded in greeting

"I'm Amanda," said the girl who had spoken first. "This is Lacy and her brother Luke. We were running a mock operation when we were grabbed." The girl with the same accent as Luke waved her hand half heartedly. She looked like Luke's twin.

"Audrey," said the red-headed Canadian with a curt nod.

"Miguel," the Mexican guy introduced himself with a nod as well.

"David," the Brazilian guy introduced himself.

" I am Victor," said the Russian a little loudly. David hushed him with a finger to his lips and a stern look.

"What a cliché name," Matt whispered in my ear.

"Now that is settled; if no one has a problem let's get started."

"I have problem," interjected Victor. "Ve are going to get ourselves killed, I rather like living. Da guards have machine guns. Dis is suicide."

"May I?" Audrey asked me with a hand reaching to my Beretta. I handed it to her. "Look, I don't know what your problem is, but if you don't follow orders, if you don't do what you're told, you will have a new problem. Namely, a bullet lodged in your foot. To start with anyway. Got it ?" Victor shrugged and shied away from the gun-wielding Canadian, but gave no further protest. We were trained to have a no-tolerance attitude when it came to disobeying orders and crybabies. I didn't agree exactly with Audrey's methods, but I couldn't argue with the result. I was starting to like her.

I nodded at Lacy to get started. She crept over to the door.

"I have to go to the bathroom!" she called loudly.

"Suck it up," came the muffled reply from the guard on the other side of the door.

"Who's job is it to clean up the mess, if I can't hold it?" asked Lacy. With some audible grumbling, the door was unlocked and swung open. David rushed the guard and had him in a chokehold before the shocked man could make a sound. I picked up the machine gun from the ground, looking up in time to see David break the guard's neck and deposit him in a dark corner of the room. He checked the guard's pockets and found a pack of cigarettes and a lighter. I wasn't planning to rack up a body count, but it was too late now. I pulled out a magazine and looked at the bullets.

"I have good news and bad news. The good news is it's unlikely that the guards will shoot us, at least with machine guns. The bad news, this gun is useless. It's loaded with blanks and the other guard had his gun on safety. I don't think he knew it either." I whispered to the operatives, and the news was met with shrugs and nods of understanding.

We all stacked up on the door, and Matt counted us off. On three, we noiselessly broke into the hall and scoped out the area. It was void of guards and had four other doors lining the hall. On the door of the holding room, a listening devise was taped. I pointed it out to the kids and moved on. There was a vent at one end of the hall, and a window with an air conditioning unit at the other. Next to one door was a huge tinted window; this had to be the interrogation room. I knew from my mental map that the one at the far end was the interrogation room I had been in, and the one next to it was the stairwell. I pulled open the door across from the holding room. It was a supply closet.

"Jackpot," I whispered mostly to myself. I pulled out an aerosol can of cleaner and a tiny tool box. I flipped open the tool box to find a screwdriver, box cutter, duct tape, a small hammer, a large heavy wench, pliers, and a tape measure. I took the aerosol can and tool box, but I left the other cleaning products, mini first aid kit, and toilet paper in the closet. We moved on to the next door.

The remaining door had a small pane of safety glass showing the room beyond. I peeked in and quickly took stock of what was inside. I could see 11 guards and the interrogator. The room was basically a break room. It had a coffee maker and small refrigerator. Tables filled the center of the room and everyone was lounging in folding chairs, smoking, and refilling coffee mugs. It had two windows that gave a beautiful view of the Hawaiian rainforest. The door wasn't locked. I backed away from the door and looked at the ceiling, thinking. The building had a false ceiling and had large moveable panels made of speckled drywall-like material.

I had an idea.

I walked over to the hall window and pulled the screwdriver from the tool box. I started to dismantle the air conditioning unit. David helped me heave it out of the window and set it on the floor. I looked at the exterior of the building. It had a wide windowsill and a gutter that was bolted to the roof. I smiled to myself. I shared my idea and the operatives got to work. Lacy and I were the smallest of the teens so we went over to the supply closet. I climbed up the shelves. Carefully pushing the false ceiling panel up and to the side, I pulled myself up and into the ceiling. I was careful not to put my weight on the panels or weak spots. I crawled along on the cross beams and pipes. When I got to the wall dividing the closet and the break room, I wrapped my legs around a pipe and pulled the box cutter from my pocket. I sawed away at the drywall and made a square hole just big enough for me and Lacy to wiggle through. I replaced the knife in my back pocket. I moved off into the next room and Lacy came up after me. I could hear them talking, but didn't concentrate on what was being said. I worked my way across the room, trying not to make a sound. Lacy had set up in the corner waiting for the signal. When I had reached the spot I had last seen a guard, I stopped and lifted a panel just enough to see below me. The guard was right where he had been 10 minutes ago; he was still drinking coffee and flirting with the attractive interrogator. He was standing near the far window with two other buddies, and the interrogator was sitting at a table nearby. I replaced the panel and my headset crackled to life.

"Window, all set," whispered Audrey over the headset.

"Door, ready," replied Matt

"Ceiling, in position, bomb's away," I answered under my breath into the headset. I pulled my Beretta from my waistband. I nodded at Lacy who pulled a flash bang from her jacket. She lifted the panel and pulled the pin of the flash bang. She threw the grenade into the room below. Lacy dropped the panel back into place, and we both closed our eyes and clamped our hands over our ears. The room shook slightly with the force of the explosion. Panic erupted under us.

"All units go," ordered Audrey. Each group attacked in the same instant. Lacy and I attacked from the ceiling. Audrey, David and Amanda from the windows and Matt, Victor and Miguel from the door.

I gave Lacy a thumbs up. I rolled my weight onto the panel, it gave under me, and I fell onto the guard's back. I wrapped one arm around his neck, locking the startled guard in a chokehold in one fluid movement. In my remaining hand, I held the Beretta and aimed over the guard's shoulder. I shot one of the guards across the room in the shoulder, causing him to drop his gun and fall to the floor. I placed another round in the leg of a guard who was trying to run. Lacy dropped from the ceiling a second after me, landing on a guard and ramming his head into the table, knocking him out.

As I fell, both windows flew open and Audrey and David rolled into the room followed by Amanda. Audrey came up behind a disoriented guard and cracked him in the temple with the wrench. David took the guard next to me and put a combat knife to his throat, the guard dropped his gun and surrendered. Amanda came up through the window with several pairs of handcuffs. She had half of the guards in chains before they knew what had happened.

With a crash, Matt, Luke, and Miguel came charging in through the door. They knocked a vacant table on its side and took cover. Peeking over the table, Matt let off three rounds. Each round hit their mark, the shoulders of two guards and the knee of a third who was seated. Miguel sprinted from cover and struck a guard in the head with the hammer, killing him. Luke hopped over the table and ran right to the interrogator, putting his combat knife to her throat; she gave up without a fight. The entire attack took only a few seconds.

With a deafening roar a hidden guard sprang from under a table and rushed Lacy. She turned and fumbled with the lighter, letting out a stream of spray from the aerosol can. At the last second the lighter flickered to life and a flaming ball of burning gas engulfed the enraged guard. He fell to the floor screaming and making failed attempts to put out the flames.

Luke splashed the interrogator's coffee on the burning guard, extinguishing the flames. Victor walked into the room after the shooting had stopped and passed the remaining handcuffs. In total, we had 8 handcuffs and 10 guards, so we chained them together. We secured the remaining guards and searched them. We laid out the contents of their pockets on the table, out of their reach. The guards were laid face down on the floor, the interrogator was duct taped to a chair.

"I have money, I can get you whatever you want," offered the interrogator desperately. Audrey slapped a piece of tape over her mouth and the interrogator's pleas were silenced.

I took out my cell phone, pressed speed dial, and handed it to David. "Get the ETA on backup," I told him. He put the phone to his ear and started talking with a handler.

"Found it!" called Miguel holding up two machine guns. "These have normal rounds."

"This one too," added Amanda, also holding a third.

"What's going on up there?" cracked a voice over a two-way radio on the table.

"Shit, they must have heard the flash bang," said Luke.

"ETA is one hour," called David hanging up the phone. One hour meant backup would be here in 20 minutes.

"Lacy, Luke, you two stay here with two machine guns. If anyone moves, shoot them," I ordered. Miguel handed off the guns. Lacy gave me the aerosol can. The rest of us filed out into the hall, leaving the siblings to look after eleven guards and one interrogator. I knew they were more than capable of keeping the remaining ten in line.

I moved over to the stairwell and cracked the reinforced door open. I found no one at the top of the stairs so I leaned a little further to see the rest of the stairs. No one was in the stairwell, just an old furnace and a wet floor sign. Suddenly the door flew open and guards rushed in. I pulled back and shut the door. The teens stacked up on the door, ready for a fire fight. I shook my head and handed off my gun to David. I held up a finger, telling them to wait. Running into the interrogation room, I picked up the metal chair and returned to the hall. I wedged it under the handle and kicked it into place, effectively sealing off the stairs. The group returned to the break room.

"Back already?" asked Lacy.

"We missed you too much," said David with a grin.

"The stairs were too hot. We have to find another way out. We can't hold up for one hour," I explained.

"You know, we are only on the second floor and there is grass down there," David coolly pointed out, looking out of the window at the ground.

"Only da second floor?" Victor repeated in outrage.

"Yeah, and we could regroup right there," said Audrey pointing to a thick section of rainforest.

"That could work, the guards are entering from the opposite side of the building. We could be gone before anyone realizes it," agreed Matt.

"First, we need to take care of them," I said jerking my thumb at the guards on the floor. David loaded a fresh clip in his gun and cocked it. Some of the guards whimpered.

"That's not what I meant," I said as I rolled my eyes. I left the room and returned with the mini first aid kit. With the help of Audrey and Amanda, I was able to patch up all the guard's major injuries. Then we carefully stamped on the back of each guards' heads, quickly knocking them out. David knocked out the interrogator with the butt of his gun.

"Ok, Matt and I will cover you from the window, Luke and Lacy can cover us on the ground," I said, taking the machine gun from Amanda.

The operatives dropped to the ground and rolled two at a time. The siblings went first, next was Miguel and David, then Audrey and Amanda, and I nodded at Matt who jumped next. I stepped up to the window to jump also, when I felt a gun barrel press into the small of my back. It was Victor and judging by the size of the barrel, he had a revolver.

Chapter 6

I let out my breath in a sigh - Victor was a mole. He was planted in the holding room by the kidnappers. It made sense now that I thought about it. Victor had wanted me to tell him what the backup plan was. He spoke too loudly when he introduced himself and didn't want us to leave the room. He wasn't trained like an operative, because he wasn't an operative. And he had caught me off guard and alone.

"Drop your gun, nice and slow," he ordered, all traces of his Russian accent gone. I let the gun fall to the floor. Sickening dread pooled in my stomach. I had made a huge mistake.

I brushed a few strands of hair over my ear, subtly turning on my headset, "You know, I would have never pegged you as a mole. You're a good actor, but not perfect."

"What do you mean?" he asked, sounding distracted.

"Your ID number was off. Everyone else is from North, South or Central America. You pretended to be Russian. Plus your accent was a tad off and your cover name was cliché," I explained, trying to buy time.

"Something to remember for next time," he told me moving the gun to the back of my head.

"There isn't going to be a next time," I assured him.

In a flourish, I grabbed his gun hand and twisted it away, chopped his elbow, and pointed the gun in his face. His eyes widened in shock and disbelief. I pushed him in a 180 turn so his back was to the window.

"Go," I said over the headset.

A hand reached up through the window and caught Victor by the shoulder and pulled him back. In surprise, Victor let go of the gun and I pulled it from his grip. He fell two stories, flailing as he went, and landed heavily on the grass below. I looked down at David who grinned up at me. He had free climbed up the side of the building. With a wink he let go and fell next to Victor and rolled. Victor let out a pitiful moan.

"Oh shut up, you big baby, you only bruised a rib or two and maybe sprained your ankle," said David to the distressed Victor. I dropped to the ground behind David.

"Nice, how did you know he was a mole?" asked Matt.

"It was pretty clear, when he put a gun to my head," I answered.

"Oh, that would give it away," nodded Matt.

"Is this the part where we get to interrogate him?" asked David.

"No, we should save that for the operatives when they get here," I told him.

The three of us knocked him out and left him on the grass. All eight teens scampered across the grass and slipped into the rainforest. From the trees, we watched as two helicopters landed and adult operatives poured out, unleashing havoc on the guards. They poured into the building from every door and window. From where we stood, I could make out some familiar faces. I saw Nick, Dimitri, Barracuda, and Leah dragging guards into one of the helicopters. Others were giving medical aid to the injured and a few cleaned up blood and wiped everything down for fingerprints. It was hard to be sure in the dark, but I thought I saw Venom, a renowned operative. He was one of the rock stars of our world. Venom was bent over the interrogator who looked scared out of her mind. All the operatives were in body armor and armed to the teeth. Everyone but one; he stepped off the helicopter last, wearing a black suit and was without visible weapons. I had never seen him before, but I felt a deep unexplainable chill when I looked at him. My phone buzzed, it was Tonya. I told her we were in the trees and everyone was in one piece.

Hours later all eight trainees sat in the Big Island Local Command Center's kitchen. It was housed under a fine jewelry store. The local operation center was much smaller in Hawaii; a large facility was unnecessary because Hawaii didn't have any large operations. After being debriefed, filling out paperwork, and being cleared by the infirmary staff, they sat talking over food.

"Can you believe the whole thing was a test? Set up and kidnapped by our own people!" said Amanda in outrage.

"Well we passed," said David unconcerned.

"I'm just glad we aren't in trouble for killing guards. They weren't operatives, just hired thugs," said Lacy.

"It still sucks to be lied to," said Luke, and we muttered in agreement.

The Local Operations Director informed us during debriefing that the kidnapping was a test, set up and controlled by the Organization. He told us that we were never in any real danger and that we all passed the test. All the guards were hired guns and the interrogator was an employee given one last chance to do something productive for the Organization. One look from the Director silenced our protests and outbursts. After debriefing, we were told to go to the infirmary then get some food and sleep. It took just under an hour for everyone to be cleared by the medical staff. Together we made a late dinner and pushed two tables together and dug in.

"No point getting worked up about it," Matt pointed out.

"Maybe it was just me, but did anyone see a guy named Venom out there?" asked Miguel changing the subject.

"I thought I saw him with the interrogator. I would love to shadow that guy for a week," I said.

"I met him once in Brasilia. He was cool, didn't say much though. He mostly just sat in the corner near the door and cleaned his gun. I never want to get on his bad side," said David.

"Have you ever heard of Samson?" asked Audrey.

"What, like the guy from the Bible?" said Amanda.

"No, Samson, the legendary operative." said Audrey rolling her eyes.

"Never heard of him," I admitted. The other kids agreed.

"He was recruited from the Marines after he finished his fourth tour. He was built like a line backer mixed with a body builder. He got the codename Samson because of his strength. Samson tore doors off their hinges, could carry several hundred pounds of equipment and armor. Once he ripped a car apart with his bare hands to save an operative. The CEO, the guy that created the Organization, made a new division just for Samson. They called it Operation Delilah, I guess someone has a sense of humor.

"They made him into a human wrecking ball. He was covered in heavy armor and carried a range of hulking automatic guns. Samson was not fast, but he didn't need to be. He had the fire power to plow through any enemy base, any mine field, and any hostile, hopeless mission. He was the guy they called to clean up a job gone bad. He, like several agents, entered the Organization because he was promised revenge.

" While on his last tour as a Marine, his pregnant wife was kidnapped. Samson's handler told him if he worked for them, they would help him get her back. Over the years, as Samson diligently held up his end of the deal, his handler told him they were getting closer to saving her. When it came time for him to step down from active duty, Samson's handler told him that they had found his wife and she was dead. He flew into a rage and killed his handler. In an attempt to cover up the murder, Samson discovered his handler had a file on his wife and unborn child. They both had been killed right after the kidnapping and the Organization knew it; they used it to manipulate him and made him work. The dead handler was found and Samson went into hiding, always hunting his family's killer.

"He swore to make the Organization pay for lying and using him. But Samson had friends in the Organization who knew what the Organization did to him and helped Samson stay one step ahead of the 'Retirement Agents' sent to kill him." said Audrey

"Wow, sad story" said Amanda finishing her dinner.

"He is still alive, he messes with operations and constantly recruits new people to his cause. His story isn't over, he is just waiting to make his move," Audrey explained.

"How did you find out?" asked Lacey.

"I traded info with a guy in Canada," explained Audrey

"That's inspiring and all but its late, I'm heading to bed," said Luke. The teens agreed and the group dissolved. Audrey and I stayed to clean up. She washed the pots and pans and I dried.

"You know, Holly, we make a good team," she commented handing me plates.

"Yeah, we kicked ass on that test," I agreed.

"I know we just met, but if you need something or want backup on a mission, I'm your girl." She said.

"Thanks and ditto, you need friends in this business, someone watching your back," I said. I put a pan away under the stove.

"You look tired, I can finish the rest. You should get to bed before you keel over," she told me, taking a pot out of my hands and putting it in the cabinet.

I thanked her again and left the kitchen. I was almost to the dorms when Emily turned the corner and blocked my path.

"Heading somewhere?" she asked, her nose was swollen and gruesome shade of black and blue but no longer taped up.

"I was going to bed. What are you doing here?" I asked her cautiously.

"They needed Barracuda to help out and I tagged along. They transferred a lot of people from LA to Hawaii," she said. "I read the skill and knowledge test results, you'er ranked number one. I decided it was the perfect opportunity to bump you from the number one spot."

"And how are you going to do that?" I asked looking amused, but I was starting to worry.

"You got a slap on the wrist for not following orders, not a big deal if that's the only trouble you got into. However, add that to assaulting a fellow trainee, then it becomes more serious," she said.

"Everyone saw you and me sparing, your broken nose is easily blamed on that fight," I told her.

"Yes, and the severity of the break was also noted when it was reset. But if we happened to meet by accident in the halls, alone, and you happened to lose your temper and break my nose again, then you would be disciplined, and you would no longer be number one," she said with a sly smile.

"But I haven't-" I started to tell her when she grabbed the door handle of a supply closet next to us and opened the door into her face. It made a sickening crunch as the bone was smashed. She closed the door and blood ran down her face.

"You will be lucky if you get another job this year. They will likely send you to anger management. Who knows, they might even throw you out of the Organization all together," she told me.

I leaned against the wall and crossed my arms, totally unconcerned by her threats of ending my career as a trainee. "Emily, there is a reason I'm number one and you're not. You are not very observant." I pointed over my shoulder to a camera mounted on the wall. It had a small green light indicating that it was on. It had recorded her slamming the door into her own face.

Chapter 7

I couldn't help but feel like I had finally won a round against Emily. The footage of Emily's self-mutilation could get her thrown out or they might not act on it at all.

I decided to put it out of my mind and head to bed. I only had a few hours till sunrise. Some sleep was better than none. I found my room, changed, and fell face first onto my pillow. Within minutes, I was out. My mind must have known how much my body needed the sleep, because the night was void of dreams, good or bad. I awoke to a soft knock at my door and Nick's voice telling me it was morning. I gave a sleepy grunt of acknowledgment. He told me everyone was in the classroom and wouldn't wait for me. I quickly changed into shorts and a blue tank top. It only took once to learn how unpleasant it was to oversleep; the usual response was a bucket of ice water over the head. I looked at the clock, it was dawn.

I dressed and dragged my half-conscious self to a small room dubbed 'the classroom'. It had several desks and white boards lining the walls. The other trainees were already seated at desks, tapping away on laptops. I took my place next to Matt and booted up my computer. I read the assignment off the board: two hours of language practice, half an hour math, half an hour of weapon recognition and a protocol quiz, a quick break for breakfast then on to marksmanship, then sparring. A busy morning. I clicked on a language program and set to work, first on French, then Spanish. Math seemed to drag on, but weapon recognition was fast paced and entertaining. My stomach growled but I pushed it out of my mind, I knew breakfast was soon. The protocol quiz was extensive and covered nearly every aspect of Organization life. When it was finally over the trainees somberly filed out of the classroom and into the kitchen. Most were vocally of the opinion that it was too early to be up.

We ate a quick meal of eggs, fruit, ham and whole grain waffles. Conversation picked up after everyone was wide awake and fed. We cleaned up our dishes and reported to the shooting range for marksmanship.

Nick ran us through drills for an hour, then dismissed us for a short break to change for sparring. I was already wearing a tank top and athletic shorts and didn't need to change, I thought up a better use of my time. I speed walked to the kitchens and dug around till I found junk food stashed behind a few cookbooks. I grabbed a chocolate bar and replaced the books.

I left the kitchen, and headed for IOC. I was halfway there when I saw Ryan, clutching his laptop and a fist full of files, walking down another hall. I followed silently after him. He entered a room marked "file storage" and I slipped in after him. The room was long and poorly lit, it was lined by fireproof filing cabinets. Ryan set his laptop down and pulled a key from his pocket. He slid the key in and unlocked a cabinet near the back of the room and started to sort files.

"Did you get demoted?" I asked. Ryan jumped, evidently he didn't hear me come in. "Filing seems a little below you".

"Shit Holly, stop sneaking up on me! What are you doing here? Filing is not your thing either," he said, picking up files he had dropped.

"I came to find you, I need a favor," I explained.

"Anything," Ryan finished stuffing files back in their places.

"I need 30 minutes with your laptop and access codes," I told him, trying to make it sound like an everyday request.

"Anything but that," he replied trying to hide his shock and busied himself with another handful of files.

"I brought payment." I held up the chocolate. He eyed it hungrily; we all lived a life without indulgences. "I just need access to information. You can get files and make it look like work."

"If this is about your mum, you're be'er off not knowing," he said.

"It's not about her it's about-" I started but was cut off.

"No, I don't even want to know." He looked at the candy bar and I knew I had him.

I shrugged. "30 minutes, that's all I need." I tossed the chocolate to him.

He ripped off the wrapper and bit in. "Almost as sweet as you, love. You have 25, I'll be in the corner."

He was behind a cabinet and across the room. I set to work. It took only seconds to find what I was looking for. I finished with 6 minutes to spare and found the personnel files. I hovered my mouse over my mother's name. It wasn't what I had come for. Did I really want to know? I wasn't even sure what I was looking for. It was likely that her file was just legend and held nothing useful at all. Maybe Ryan was right and I needed to move on. Living in someone else's shadow could be maddening. But even so she was my mother and I had a right to know. The clock was ticking and I had to choose. I wasn't going to get another chance like this for a long time. I clicked on her name and speed-read the file. I knew most of it by heart, from stories and rumors. Nothing was said about me other than that she had a child. I was about to give up when I saw a name: Epsilon. He was her partner. I quickly found his file and speed-read through it. They were partners for 7 years and worked flawlessly together. After he was killed in action and my mother refused time off, she took her last mission. There was no mention as to the mission's purpose, but it was her last. I was starting to put together a time line but it was incomplete and I still didn't know where I fit in. I pulled up the report on Epsilon's death, but I was denied access. Ryan didn't have high enough clearance. I went back to the personnel files and looked up a few more people.

After exactly 25 minutes Ryan walked back to where I sat, just as I finished wiping traces of my activity from his computer.

"Pleasure doing business with you," I said as I left the room.

He nodded his head, probably wondering if he should regret what just happened.

I hated using Ryan like that, but what I just set up would likely save my life one day.

I set off down the hall to sparring. I had just passed the door to the IOC when the door opened and the Hawaiian Head of Operations Director stepped into the hall.

"Holly, please come with me," he said holding the door open for me. I carefully placed a curious and slightly surprised expression on my face. I entered the IOC, he followed and closed the door behind us. I had underestimated the Organization. It had taken them just minutes to spot what I did on Ryan's computer. I was astounded that they could work that fast. Maybe Ryan's computer was being watched already, or maybe he turned me in the second I left the room. Either way I was in big trouble.

Chapter 8

I stepped into the Director's office and sat in the chair in front of his desk. He took his seat and typed on the desktop computer before him. He was much younger than the LA local Director. He was thinner, tanner and appeared overall healthier. The office smelled like paper and leather rather than smoke. A subtle bulge on the right side of his waist indicated a sidearm. He was clean shaven and had a kind face. He tapped "enter" on the computer and I could hear Tonya's voice on the line.

Shit, I was really in trouble if I had to talk to my handler and the Director.

"Hello, Holly" She said with a pleasant voice. "I assume you know what this is about".

I shook my head, working hard not to give myself away.

"The Director and I have analyzed the reports from your test and we feel your outstanding leadership has proven you capable of handling more responsibility. It has been decided that you and Matt no longer need to be trainees and as of now, you are promoted to first echelon operative and will be assigned an upper echelon operative to shadow and assist," Tonya said. The Director nodded his agreement.

Despite my best efforts my jaw dropped. I was so sure I was going to get an earful of protocol and rules. Instead I was being promoted. I tried to say something but couldn't. The dread that had taken up residence in the pit of my stomach had turned to shock, confusion and suspicion.

"You and Matt will be stationed here in Hawaii," explained the Director. "We have a operation in play and need a few more people

in the field. LA doesn't have any current major projects so many of
its operatives have been moved here and promoted. You will get your
assignments tomorrow," the Director continued. I nodded, it was all I
could manage.

"Now that you're an agent, you will need a gun. A safety deposit
box was recovered recently. It belonged to an operative you knew,
Brigit. She won't be needing the contents and it seemed fitting that you
should inherit them," said Tonya. The Director picked up a thick manila
envelope and handed it to me.

Pulling out my switch blade I slit open the envelope and slid the
contents into my lap. The largest of objects was a 9 mm Glock 2k12 with
a high-capacity magazine full of ammo. The gun was entirely matte black
and had a detachable silencer, scope and laser dot projector. I picked it
up, it was perfectly weighted and fit my hand like it was made for me.
Holding my mother's gun made her somehow more real. I set the gun
on the desk and held up a locket. It was silver and had Arabic writing on
it. Next was a set of colored contacts along with a small, worn picture
depicting a mother and child. I had to fight to keep my composure. At
the bottom of the pile was a letter addressed to me. I turned it over to
open it but it was already cut … of course.

"Naturally the letter has been read and censored. The box also had
passports and files that would be useless to you so we disposed of them
to save you the trouble," explained the Director.

"Naturally," I agreed, hiding my disappointment as I felt my heart
slide into my stomach. I scooped everything back into the envelope.
"Should I go back to sparring or is there something else?" I asked, in a
flat tone, still stuffing my emotions.

"No, you need to go to the armory and get outfitted. Then go to the
dining room and meet your mentor. You will be shadowing Onyx. She
is not in yet, but should be by the time you're done at the armory," he
explained.

I nodded and got up to leave.

"At the risk of sounding cliché, with this new freedom comes more
responsibly. Consequences for your actions, like disobeying orders, will
become more severe," warned Tonya.

"Yes ma'am," I acknowledged. I left the office and walked to the
armory holding my inheritance.

The door to the armory was heavy and reinforced. I pushed the door open. The interior was large and looked like a cross between a warehouse and a gun shop. I walked to the counter and stood in front of a large red-faced man, about middle age, who was cleaning a shotgun. I placed my envelope on the counter and he looked up.

"How can I help you kid, running an errand for your mentor?" he asked, putting the shotgun down.

"No sir, I was told to come and get outfitted," I explained.

He smiled kindly. "I take it you were just made an agent? Congrats! You will be needing your first gun and plenty of ammo. You'll need a running suit and headset too..." he trailed off making a list in his head.

"I already have a gun and full clip." I pulled my Glock out to show him. He took it gently from my hand and examined it with fatherly patience. He disassembled the gun with fluid ease.

"Good God, I bet you have no idea what you have here," he gasped at the gun in amazement. "What did you do to earn this little prize?" I shrugged noncommittal.

"What you have here is a Glock 2k12 and extended magazine. You feel how warm it is? How it's not as cold as metal? That's because it's made of high impact plastic. It can go through metal detectors, makes airport security less…exciting. The silencer is custom too. But the coolest thing is this…" he flipped on a switch near the safety and the gun flickered before my eyes and suddenly took on the color of the counter behind it. The gun had active camo. I glanced up at the master of arms in shock. He could hardly contain his enthusiasm. "The plastic is coated on the outside with a pattern of color-sensing micro-beads and micro-beads that change color depending on the current running through 'em! So the gun can turn virtually invisible!" he explained, rocking back and forth on the balls of his feet. I couldn't help wonder how the hell my mother had come to own a gun like that.

The master of arms handed me an extra clip, some 9mm ammo and a holster for my Glock. He quickly measured me for my running suit, which would be custom-fit and delivered later. I thanked him and left the armory. I felt better with my mother's gun in its new holster. I walked down the hall ready to meet my mentor.

Glancing around as I stepped into the dining hall I found Onyx easily enough. She was taller than me at about 5'5". Her black hair was cropped short and her bangs covered one eye. Her skin was dark and hinted that she had one black parent and one white. She sat with her back to the wall, brown eyes scanning the room ceaselessly. She picked at the food in front of her with one hand while twirling a throwing knife in the other. She looked bored and relaxed but ready for action if necessary. I noticed everyone in the room gave her a wide berth. She looked me up and down as I entered the room, her gaze lingered for a second on my holster gun. I grabbed a plate of chicken and rice and sat across from her.

"You would be Holly" she said in a slightly bemused tone.

"And you would be Onyx," I said. She set down her fork to shake my hand. The knife never left her long fingers.

"Is that your first gun?" she asked. I unholstered my gun and passed it to her. She looked it over and passed it back. "Funny they would give you her last gun," she said quietly as if she was talking to herself.

"You knew my mother?" I asked in surprise. I watched the light glint off the knife as it spun faster.

"I worked with her, only a few times though. We both had our own partners and it was rare that all four of us were needed," she explained. Onyx stopped scanning, her eyes were fixed on something over my shoulder. "But your mother was one hell of an agent," she added with a almost sentimental air.

"I'll drink to that" said a deeper voice behind me. I looked around to see the newcomer. Venom slid into the chair next to Onyx and set a bottle of whisky and two glasses down.

"You would drink to anything," Onyx said with an ornery grin.

"Your point?" Venom grinned back and poured out a measure of whisky in each glass. He passed one glass to Onyx, who accepted it but didn't drink. Venom's appearance lived up to the rumors of being an ex-US Marine. He was tall at 6' 4" with arms covered with tattoos. Venom had a commanding presence and radiated power. "So who are we drinking to?" He raised a glass to his lips still grinning, his eyes on Onyx.

"Bridget," I answered.

The smile slid off his face. "Damn shame about Bridget, she was so careful, I thought she would outlive us all. Though she did go kind of funny in the end-" Venom was cut off by Onyx who elbowed him in the ribs. Onyx nodded pointedly towards me and resumed scanning. Venom looked me over carefully, his eyes widening as he recognized who I was. "You would be her daughter, you look just like her you know. Sorry, I didn't realize that you..." He trailed off.

"Don't worry about it," I told him.

Onyx's eyes paused on something over my shoulder. I turned to look at whatever had caught her attention this time. Matt was making his way over with a plate of chicken and rice as well as two empty glasses.

"Hey, Holly," he said in greeting. He took the chair next to me and pushed the two glasses across the table to Venom.

"Took you long enough, kid, did you get lost on your way to the armory?" asked Venom filling the two empty glasses with whisky.

"Sorry sir, the arms master had a lot to say about my gun," explained Matt.

It hit me with a sudden realization, Venom was Matt's mentor. It would make a lot of sense for Venom and Onyx to be partners like Matt and I. "You two wouldn't happen to be partners, would you?" I asked.

"Yeah, as of two weeks ago, how did you know?" confirmed Venom.

"Just a gut feeling," I said dismissively. "Didn't you have partners before each other?"

"I work solo most of the time but occasionally they match me up for specific jobs; and Onyx's partner had her brain blown out three weeks ago by a sniper in Israel," explained Venom nonchalantly. He passed Matt and I a glass of whisky each. I followed Onyx's lead and accepted it but didn't drink. Matt, however, took his and sampled it. I shot him a look to remind him he was under age and shouldn't be drinking. Venom saw my disapproval and offered his unsolicited opinion.

"If you kids are old enough to work alongside us, fight with us, and die with us, you are old enough to drink with us. If he wants some whisky, let him have it. It's not like anyone in this business lives long enough to have to worry about liver problems," he said.

"On the other hand it's hard to run for your life when you have a hangover or are completely shit-faced," pointed out Onyx. "But enough of that, I can see you have questions and odds are we have answers."

"Yeah, I do. Do you know how my mom got her start?" I asked continuing to eat.

"She told me once. Bridget was the daughter of an IRA recruiter and an undercover Scotland Yard detective, neither knew about the other's real occupation. They lived in Belfast and were happy for a long time. Each parent taught her a little of their art and beliefs and such. Inevitably the truth came out and they blew each other to hell over it, leaving a teenage Bridget orphaned. The Organization offered her a place to use her skills and vent her anger over her dead family. She joined up because the IRA came knocking, and joining them would have felt like betrayal to one parent and joining the police would have felt like betraying the other," Onyx recounted. Then she warned, "But keep it to yourself, you kids aren't supposed to know."

My phone buzzed and I flipped it open to look at the text massage. Matt, Onyx and Venom did the same. All four of us got to our feet, and I assumed their message was similar. Mine said simply: report to the briefing room ASAP, timetables have changed. Your first mission starts now -Tonya.

Chapter 9

Everything that had happened in my life led up to this assignment. Years of training, my test/kidnapping, my new promotion, my new gun and inheritance was preparation for this. Whatever it was, this job was high enough profile that the Organization would be willing to bring in kids.

The briefing room was large enough to accommodate 20 or so people. Dominating the center of the room was a large oval table encircled with black business-like chairs. Manila envelopes were placed in front of each seat with an agent's ID number printed at the top. I took my place next to Onyx and eyed my envelope wondering what it could contain. I turned my attention to the Director standing at the head of the table next to a large projector screen.

"We just received intel on Lloyds of London, a massive insurance company. One of their clients has taken a one billion dollar insurance policy on an object. It's being transported by boat from Hawaii to Mexico. The boat hasn't left yet, giving us time for a little recon. Lloyds of London has decided that it's cheaper to hire a black ops team to guard the object, rather than take the risk of paying out one billion US dollars. Naturally the Organization has decided that the object is a high priority and is sending in all of you to take it," he explained. "Here's the plan. The ship's cook has been poisoned while shopping for fresh produce. He will become sick at sea and they will have to call the Coast Guard for an emergency medical rescue. Those of you in WET works will be responding to that call. We have an inside man on the black ops team who make things run smoothly. Lethal force is authorized. The entire black ops team, other than our man, must be eliminated quickly and quietly. You may rough up but not kill the crew. You have been given evidence to plant on the ship to blame a political group that the client has had trouble with in the past. Because of the shortage of manpower, two new agents are being brought in as support," he nodded to Matt and me, then continued. "Your individual information is in your envelopes. All of you will start gathering intel tonight. Good luck, don't make a mess, and come back in one piece." All the agents stood and left the room carrying their assignments. I headed to the garage with the others, but Onyx stopped me.

"We never leave all at once, you have a few minutes to pack your bag. You are rooming with me in my apartment on the east side of the island. Go grab your stuff, I'll wait," she explained and moved off to talk with a few of the other agents.

I nodded and ran to my room to gather my things. I shoved everything into my black duffle bag, my clothes, laptop, inheritance, MP3 player, and multi-tool, and finally hefted my worldly possessions over my shoulder. Rather than going straight to the garage, I took a quick detour through the training hall. I checked the classroom, the weight room, and the shooting range, each was empty. I tried the sparring room at the end of the hall and found Nick, Dimitri, Barracuda and Emily. The twins were coaching Emily on how to take Barracuda down. Dimitri looked around when I opened the door.

"Hey kid, better hurry or Onyx will take off without you," Dimitri warned.

"You already heard?" I asked mildly surprised. Although it made sense now that I thought about it, the Director would tell Nick that I had been promoted, and Nick would tell his brother.

"Yup, I'm informed like that. Are you here to say good bye?" he asked.

"Something like that," I said with half grin. "Where are the others?" directing the question at Nick.

"The kids were shipped home, back to their trainers," Nick explained. He crossed the room and pulling me into a hug. "I'm proud of you. Just be careful. Now get going before you're late," he whispered into my ear. He gently pushed me out the door and started to close it. Just before it shut Dimitri yelled his farewell. "Don't get yourself killed, kid!" I couldn't help but grin at the contrast between brothers.

The goodbye was bitter sweet. Nick was the closest thing I ever had to a father and Dimitri was like an uncle. I was proud to be moving up, even if it was rushed by an understaffed operation; at the same time I didn't know when I would be seeing either of them again. They were both assigned to the new mission, otherwise they would have been left in LA, but it was possible to work the same mission and not see them at all. This thought seemed to suck my heart into the pit of my stomach. I pushed it out of my mind and hurried off to meet Onyx.

****

We drove to Hilo, on the northeastern side of the Big Island, in two separate cars. The two bedroom apartment, across from the University of Hawaii, was small and cramped with four people. I shared a room with Onyx and Matt shared one with Venom. It was near Hilo Bay and the yacht transporting the one billion dollar insured object.

Once inside I took my duffle bag to the girl's room to put in the closet. I slid open the door and found clothes already there. Half of the clothes there were exactly my size. I found several pairs of bikinis, tank tops and shorts, ranging from tourist to local styles and a wide selection of shoes, also exactly my size. The other half was slightly larger, I assumed they were for Onyx. It was a little unnerving that the Organization knew my shirt, pant, shoe, even bra size. I set my bag inside and slid the door closed.

I sat at the tiny kitchen table with my manila envelope, a pad of paper and pen to take notes. I slit open the top with my switchblade and spread the contents out in front of me. Yacht blueprints, time tables, ship manifests, a map of Hilo Bay, and a new cell phone, looked back at me. I started with the typed-up orders detailing what I was expected to do each day, where and when. Tomorrow I was on a stakeout, watching any activity on the yacht and make hourly reports by cell phone. The next day I was to be Onyx's backup on her assignment. I quickly studied the pictures of the yacht and put the papers back in the file. I tucked the file and my phone in my bag and got ready for bed.

It had been a long day, what with training, the promotion, the new assignment and saying good bye to Nick and all. I was exhausted but the tiny apartment was alive with noises that I had never heard sleeping several stories underground in the complex. The sound of the next door neighbor's TV floated into the room through the thin walls. I could hear Onyx breathing in the bed next to mine. I tried to focus and will myself to sleep. After what felt like hours I finally drifted off to sleep.

I found myself on the roof of the apartment where I was living back in LA. It was late at night; the city was lighting up all around me. It was cold but it felt good after the hard workout Nick had just put Matt and me through. I was stretched out on my stomach next to Matt. We chatted about everything, mostly venting about the day. Conversation came easy and we ended up talking about our childhood. I didn't have much to tell, it had always been my mom and me against the world. Matt had a very different upbringing.

He was born on Fort Lewis, Washington, to an air force captain father and a civilian mother. The happy family of three moved around together from base to base. In 1999 Matt's father was shipped off to fight in Operation Noble Anvil. His mother had waited for him to come home for months, when two uniformed Airmen knocked on her front door. She started crying the second she saw them. Matt watched from the hall as they told his mother that the helicopter was shot down and his father was killed. Matt was six at the time. Fast-forward eight years to find Matt in military school with a I-just-don't-care attitude and a talented marksman. He was pulled out of class, told that his mother had just been pronounced dead after she was hit by a drunk driver. Matt told me he felt numb, he was completely in shock. In the middle of the night the shock turned to rage; he ran away from the school looking for some way to vent and find a cause. One of the Organization's many recruiting agents found him and gave him something to care about. Something worth his time and talent with a gun. What that was I didn't know, but I suspected it was revenge.

A loud buzzing sound brought me back to consciousness. A beautiful Hawaiian sunrise was fighting its way into the room though the thick blinds. Onyx beat me to the alarm clock between our beds. She checked her phone and then crossed to the window. She peered out the window without moving the blinds. Onyx turned back towards me as I sat up and pushed my hair out of my face.

"Up for a little run?' she asked.

"Sure, I don't have to start my surveillance till 7," I answered looking at the clock. It was 5 am. Oh well, it's not like I was going to learn anything from my mentor asleep.

Several miles later and a few pounds in water weight lighter I had effectively worked out for the day. I showered and ate a light breakfast. In my room, sitting on my bed, was a package addressed to me. I slit it open with Onyx's permission to find a Naniloa Volcanoes Resort room key card. My cell phone chirped in my pocket, informing me that my handler had just texted me. I flipped it open and read the detailed instructions for the day's assignment.

I quickly dressed in a bikini under a tank top and jean shorts, oversized sunglasses, a pink sun hat, and flip flops. I tried to pick something that both blended in with the other teen age tourists and wear something that I could go in the water with, if necessary. Sunglasses could hide where I was looking if someone got nosey enough to notice. The outfit wouldn't restrict my ability to free run like a sundress would. Plus, I looked good in it. Unfortunately, it was all tight fitting and no place to hide a gun on my person.

I dug around in the closet till I found a beach bag and filled it with my gun, camera, phone, key card and a towel to hide it all under. I walked to the tiny kitchen to tell Onyx that I was heading out, but she had already left. I walked the mile and a half to the resort in the gorgeous Hawaiian weather. After darting through the lobby, I took the stairs up to the eleventh floor. I walked with my head down through the halls, using my hat to hide my face from the cameras and tourists. I found the right room number and swiped the card while putting my hand on my gun in my bag. Carefully easing the door open I found the room occupied by a very bored looking Matt. I hadn't seen him since last night. He jumped up from the chair when I came in.

"Crap, what time is it?" he asked panicking.

"Hello to you too, Matt," I replied. "It's seven, why?"

"Because I am supposed to meet Venom in five minutes," he explained, grabbing his back pack and heading to the door. "The list of things I touched is on the table. Would you mind wiping down for me?" he asked.

"Sure, see you later," I called after him as he left the room.

The room had a single king-sized bed, a small table, and most importantly, a balcony that had a perfect view of the target. I grabbed a wet wipe off the table and started wiping down all the things that he had touched, crossing each one off the list as I went. With that finished, I went onto the balcony and over to the lounge chair with my bag. I popped in my head phones and laid back with the new camera and huge lens, ready for a long wait.

The Organization doesn't fire people. Option one, they retire them: they live out their life performing the occasional minor mission and living comfortably on an allowance from the Organization. Option two, if they screw up they can be sent on a seemingly never-ending stretch of stakeout and surveillance jobs. Option three, they can be "fired", or killed but never officially and no one ever admits it. The reason the Organization uses stakeouts as punishment is because its painfully boring and usually very long. In my case it was all day, which was still better than weeks on end.

I spent hours watching the boat through the lens of the camera as it gently bobbed up and down in Hilo Bay, reporting in every hour on the hour through text on a burn phone. I took short breaks to get water and apply sunscreen. LA was hot, but not like Hawaii at noon. I got hungry and ordered room service with permission from Tonya. I stepped into the bathroom and turned on the shower, so as to avoid the hotel staff. They left the food by the door and departed. I ate and went back to the balcony. A large cruise ship pulled up at a different dock, nearly obscuring my view of the yacht. People poured out in flamboyant touristy clothes, but none went near the target. Trucks and dock workers rushed in and out loading and unloading cargo ships. Huge metal containers were stacked in the blistering sun. It's funny how time passes slowly when you're doing something so mind-numbingly dull as staring at an inanimate object all day. Hours passed and still no action. I ordered more food and ran though just about every play list I had on my mp3 player.

I was pretty sure nothing was going to happen, when I saw four men get out of a white pickup truck and walk over to the yacht. I scrambled to set up the laser microphone that Matt had left in the hotel room. I pointed it at the window hoping to catch something. I pulled on the mic's headphones and snapped off a picture of each man as they boarded the yacht.

"Is it big enough?" said one waving a hand at the 150 foot yacht.

"I have no doubt that it's sea worthy, I just don't like transporting valuables in something so conspicuous," said another.

"Well, it's what the client wants," dismissed the third.

"I don't care what he wants, our job is to keep our employer happy and-" said the second.

"And he stayed in business by keeping the client happy," interrupted the third.

"It's stupid not to fly there, it would take less time and money and be safer," said the second.

"You're paid to guard, not think," quipped the first.

"Shut up and finish the prep work so we can go," said the fourth.

They moved below and I lost the conversation. I flipped open my phone and told Tonya. After recounting what had been said she ordered me to sit tight and keep watching. She was sending in someone to tail them back. I agreed and she hung up. Five minutes later they filed out and back into the white truck. They pulled out of the lot, sped away on Kuhio Street and turned and disappeared out of sight on Kalanianaole Avenue. The tail must have been really good because I never saw one. Tonya called me back and told me to clean the room and pack everything up. That was what they were waiting for, they didn't need me there anymore. I was to meet Onyx at the apartment. Just like Matt, I had been keeping a list of everything I had touched and wiped the room down again. I broke down the mic and packed everything in my bag. I left the hotel the same way I came.

I walked back to the tiny apartment, the sun was setting, lighting the sky in different hues of orange and pink. As it turns out, Hawaiian sunsets really are all they're cracked up to be. The heat ebbed away leaving the evening cooler, but still warm enough to walk around in shorts and a tank top. I would really miss Hawaii.

I found the apartment full of activity, everyone was packing their go bags and wiping down the rooms. Onyx explained that the guards had spotted the tail and were moving the object that night rather than waiting two more days. I gathered my things and followed Matt into the car, exchanging unsure but excited looks. This was it.

Chapter 10

My senses were on over-drive as we flew in a rescue helicopter over the waves of the Pacific Ocean. The only thing louder than the helicopter's engine and blades cutting the air, was the pounding of my heart in my ears. Adrenaline and endorphins flooded my system, I had never felt so alive. Strapped in was Matt, Onyx, Venom, Notch, an extraction expert, and I, all wearing Coast Guard uniforms. Notch was another adult agent. He had an ex-military look to him and said little to anyone. He didn't have the same fame as Onyx or Venom but he out-ranked Matt and I. Everyone but the extraction guy were in full WET team gear under our uniforms. The helicopter was equipped with broad band radio jammers but they were turned off for now to avoid suspicion.

I had gone over the plan in my head a million times on the ride out. I knew what to do. But actually doing it was another matter entirely. The yacht was stopped, waiting for us as it rocked in the waves. We could see 3 out of 6 of the ops team on the top deck and two members of the crew crowded around the prone form of the ill cook.

"Try not to die, kid," Onyx whispered into my ear as we landed on the large aft deck.

I nodded and unbuckled my safety straps, we poured out onto the deck. Onyx and I went to check the cook as the others interviewed the crew. A few feet away from me, Venom and Matt tried to question some of the ops team, but they refused to talk. Out of the corner of my eye I saw one of them discretely place his gun on the deck and back up a step.

"Go," Tonya said in my head set.

The WET works team moved as one, drawing silenced weapons in unison. We had the element of surprise and two of the black ops men dead before the crew knew what happened. By putting his gun on the ground the third had shown that he was the inside man, and was left standing. Notch turned and put a round in each civilian's head.

"Top deck cleared" reported Onyx into her head set. "Two ops and three crew down"

"I thought there was a no-kill order on civilians," I said to Notch, horrified.

"They can ID us," he explained without remorse.

My headset cracked to life again. "Move out," Tonya ordered.

Venom, Matt, Notch and the inside man with his gun ducked below deck and out of sight. Onyx stayed to cover the top deck and I crept into the bridge.

The helmsman was bent over the monitor reading the heading, unaware of death outside. He turned as I entered.

"Excuse me sir, I need to interview everyone on board this vessel," I explained as I walked up to him.

In less than a second I had side-stepped him, knocked his knees out from under him and put him in a choke hold. He fought back for just over a minute. I timed it carefully to knock him out but not kill him. Once he was out I gently laid him on the deck and pulled a flash drive from my pocket. I plugged it into the main navigation computer. Tonya's voice was replaced by Ryan's as he walked me through what to do on the computer. He had been promoted to Tech Assistant and was assigned to our team. He guided me through steps to reprogram the ship's destination, sending it to a different port in Mexico. He also remotely crippled their communications.

"Done," I told him after completing the last step.

"Roger, hijacking their main frame," replied Ryan over the headset.

"Top deck cleared," reported Venom several decks below.

"Acknowledged, move aft to stairwell, then fore to galley," ordered his handler.

A few seconds later the sound of automatic gunfire erupted from one floor below. All the agents had silenced hand guns. It looked like the element of surprise was up.

"Contact in stairwell! Taking fire!" Yelled Venom.

"I'm hit!" said Notch in pained tones.

"GSW, right shoulder, through and through," reported Matt a little panicked.

"Onyx, move towards the bow and use the galley window to take out hostiles," said her handler.

"Holly, hold the bridge and top deck," ordered Tonya.

I scrambled out of the bridge and stood on the top deck so I had a good vantage point.

"Two hostiles eliminated," reported Onyx in a clinical tone.

"Proceed down to crew quarters," ordered his handler.

"Matt, stay with Notch and keep pressure on the wound," said Tonya.

"Venom, Onyx, continue down to the next deck," commanded their handler.

The ship bucked in the waves and I had to clutch the door of the bridge behind me to stay up.

"Dining room and salon cleared," reported Venom.

"The head is clear," reported Onyx.

"Matt, move Notch up to the top deck for extraction," ordered Tonya. I heard Notch grunt in pain.

I held my breath feeling useless so far from the action. From the blueprints I had memorized I knew the package should be stored just beyond the bathrooms or "head". We almost had it, whatever it was.

One deck below me Matt staggered through the door from the galley with Notch across his back in fireman's carry. He laid Notch down and pulled gauze from his small first aid kit. About ten feet behind him a large figure wriggled silently out of an access hatch. It looked like our team had missed one guard. Matt was focused on Notch's bleeding shoulder and didn't see the mercenary draw his gun.

There had been a few things I had seen while training to be an agent, some horrifying and some breathtakingly beautiful. Watching your best friend about to get his brain blown out is a sight that sticks with you. Whether you want the memory or not it burrows its way into your mind and doesn't leave.

Without thinking about it, or really realizing what I was doing, I lowered my stance and drew my own gun. I lined up the shot like I had millions of times in the shooting range. The feeling was so familiar it was almost second nature. I exhaled and squeezed the trigger. I heard the suppressed bang of the silenced gun, but the mercenary was unharmed. A tiny lever inside the gun kicked the dud bullet out of the chamber. The mercenary crept closer to Matt. In a panic I squeezed the trigger again and again. Two more duds fell to the ground. As though in slow motion I watched the mercenary take his stance, executioner style. I didn't have any throwing knives and I was too far away for hand to hand. It was too late to warn Matt of the danger behind him, he wouldn't have time to react. I couldn't breathe. All I could think was I couldn't lose Matt. In desperation I let off one more round, cursing myself for not testing my new gun before this mission. The bullet left the chamber and flew though the cold salty air, right into the center of the mercenary's forehead. I blew out the breath I had been holding and slumped onto the deck. Matt wheeled around in time to see the man's body hit the deck. The whole thing had taken only seconds.

"One hostile eliminated," I said breathlessly over my headset.

"Acknowledged, get Notch on the chopper. Time is running out," ordered Tonya.

I climbed down to my fellow agents. Matt was still by Notch, trying to stop the bleeding. Notch looked pale and a thin sheen of sweat covered his face. Matt and I gingerly lifted him up and made our way to the helicopter.

"We have the package, it seems to be intact," said Venom.

"No, wait, don't touch it!" cried Onyx. "It looks like a wire hooked up to a bomb!" and as a side note she added, "I guess they thought if they can't have it no one can."

"Send me a picture on your phone," said her handler.

I slid the door to the helicopter open and we eased Notch inside.

"Ok, it's real simple. Reach in and grab ahold of the black square, it's the detonator. Pop it open and get a picture of the wiring," said a new voice, probably some bomb expert.

Matt strapped Notch in while I turned to cover top side.

"Alright, just cut the large black wire that is soldered to the red chamber. That should do it. The light will still be on but it won't be able to start," explained the bomb expert.

The inside man returned through the door from the galley and crossed the deck to the helicopter.

"Done, I am cutting the wire now," said Onyx.

The silence over the radio told me that everyone was waiting to see if we all blew up or not. I stood with the inside man, not knowing if I was going to get the chance to take another breath.

The ship bucked again on a large swell and I prayed it didn't trigger the bomb.

"We're good," said Venom, his voice heavy with relief.

It took me a second to get my heart rate back to normal.

"Prep for evac now," said a handler in efficient tones. The helicopter started up.

Onyx stepped though the door from the lower decks, followed by her partner. Venom had a human figure across his back in a fireman's carry.

"Ladies and Gents, meet the man with a one billion dollar life insurance policy, courtesy of Lloyds of London," announced Venom, answering the confused looks on Matt's face and mine.

Fighting the force of the air from the helicopter's blades we all loaded in. Onyx took the inside man's gun as he moved to join us. She casually put a round in his leg. He fell back, clutching his thigh and looked at her in shock.

"Sorry friend, to keep your cover with London you need to look like you fought. It won't do to have you disappearing into the night with the rest of us," she yelled over the noise of the helicopter.

"We're clear," said the extraction expert into a hand held radio. The helicopter lifted into the air and flew away from the yacht.

Then the exhilaration of surviving all that hit me. The salty air whipped my hair and I felt breathless, but I lived. I more than lived, I completed my first mission perfectly.

Chapter 11

After landing in Hawaii, the following plane ride felt mind-numbingly boring in comparison to the mission. It was a private jet hired to transport our new companion to a safe location. No one knew where we were going but the pilot and copilot. We had left Notch back in Hawaii to get medical attention. Dragging a bleeding guy around a private airport tends to attract an unpleasant kind of attention. The man with the one billion dollar life insurance hadn't said a word to any of us, but oddly he didn't seem to be surprised or upset by his abduction. Then again he was strapped to a bomb on the ship and we hadn't so much as pointed a gun at him.

The team had been up all night and I hadn't slept for more than sixteen hours. I offered to take the first shift watching our friend so the others could sleep. Venom and Onyx looked even more tired than I felt, though I knew they could take it. Onyx said she didn't think anything would happen but it would be sloppy not to have someone watching the man.

I sat in a leather arm chair across from the sleeping billion dollar man. He certainly didn't look like he was worth a billion dollars. He was a scrawny middle-aged black man with wire rimmed glasses. He looked fragile and tired. The only valuable thing he could have is information. One billion dollars worth of information, and the Organization wasn't the only one to know it's potential.

My go bag was at my feet. I didn't have time before to look over my inheritance. I set the locket, contacts, picture and letter on a small table next to me. First I looked over the small silver locket. It was old and had a thin layer of tarnish. The Arabic writing was on one side, it wasn't professionally engraved, it looked like it had been scratched in by hand. The letters looked like a slanted "L", "i" and "s". Not being able to read Arabic I decided to look it up. I pulled out my computer and booted it up. I typed the letters into an online translator, the name "Hanna" popped up in the English box. It was a name that I had almost forgotten, certainly one that I hadn't heard in a decade and believed that I would never hear it again.

Frustrated at the dead end I clasped the locket around my neck and moved on to the letter.

Dear H-----,

I am writing to you because I'm afraid our time together is running out. For six years I have been on the run with you, trying to stay alive and stay free. We are running out of money and places to hide. Despite all the fear and pain, being able to hold you knowing we were together for one more day made it all worth it.

There is so much I want to tell you I don't even know where to begin. I want you to know the ----- ----- --- ------. Things are not always as they seem. The ------------- ---- --- ----------. I have a stash hidden in -----. It has ----- on --------- and -------- --- ---- -- ----.You should know ---- ------ is --- --------- -- the -----------. I never intended -- --- --- -------- --- ----. Please know I love you with all my heart.

-Bridget

I willed myself not to cry. It was the only thing my mother had written me and the Organization had taken pieces of it away with the simple stroke of a black pen. I carefully folded up the letter and slipped it into my pocket. My fingers brushed the cold dud bullets still in my pocket. I pulled them out and looked at them. As I rolled them across my palm the back of one fell off. There was a piece of paper tucked inside. I unfurled it and read it:

My real stash is in a safety deposit box in Paris.

I quickly pried the back of the second bullet and read the note inside. It was the bank address in Paris.

I eagerly opened the third and read: The key is in my old apartment, followed by an apartment address in Montreuil, France.

Ingenious, who would have thought to pass a message along in a bullet. She must have known that they would read the letter so she found a way to pass on information without the Organization knowing about it.

Venom tapped me on the shoulder, making me jump. He jerked his thumb towards the back of the plane, indicating that he was relieving me and I should vacate the chair. I gathered my things and squeezed passed him in the tiny aisle. Matt was sound asleep in a chair by a window. The exhaustion that comes after an adrenaline high of a major operation is both mental and physical. I slumped into the chair next to him and closed my eyes for a second. Before I knew it I was out.

The jarring of the plane landing woke me. I had slid sideways in my sleep so that my head rested against Matt's shoulder. His arm was around my waist. I was shocked at his uncharacteristic show of affection. I shyly gave him a quick kiss on the cheek before I pulled away and gathered my things then followed the other operatives off the plane. Matt followed sheepishly behind.

Our group marched across the small private airport and into two identical black SUVs waiting by the road. The heat created tiny mirages across the runway. We drove though an industrial district and turned into a steel mill. The SUVs drove up to the back of the main building. The first car entered into a lift large enough to easily hold a large truck. Silently the lift descended, lowering the car into an underground parking garage. The second car followed down the lift. They parked side by side next to another four identical black SUVs. Everyone wordlessly filed out of the cars and closed into formation around the mystery man. We worked our way though the underground compound. The layout was unique and I was totally lost. Venom was in front and led the pack though the labyrinth-like hide-out. It took me a few seconds to notice a faint voice coming from an ear piece in Venom's left ear. His handler was guiding him. It seemed as though none of us had any idea where we were or where we were going.

The group ended up at a large metal door that slid open as we approached. Behind the security door there was a huge cavernous tech lab. I scanned the area twice, once to check for potential threats and again to take in all the cutting edge weaponry and next generation spy equipment.

Venom stepped in first and I tried to follow but Onyx held me back. The man followed Venom inside and the door slid shut.

"What do we do now?" I asked Onyx.

"Shower, eat and sleep" she answered in a bored tone. She pulled out her phone and scrolled though a message. "This way". She walked down the hall and guided us through the maze of halls and doors, occasionally checking her phone for instructions. We ended up at a section of living quarters. After a quick shower and change of clothes Onyx led us to a dining hall. Venom had beat us there and was tearing into a large plate of pasta. I grabbed a plate and sat next to him. Matt and Onyx followed suit. We all tucked our go bags under the table, out of sight but easily accessible.

"Did you learn anything about the man?" asked Matt.

Venom raised his eyebrows, amused by Matt's eagerness for information. He slowly finished his bite and took a drink of water. "I overheard them talking while I was on guard duty. He is a programmer. They want him to build a perfect encryption code, called the Quantum Code. Apparently he came up with the theory in college."

"Venom, you should keep that to yourself. Loose lips sink ships." Onyx warned.

"Everybody wants their kids to get ahead," Venom said. "Besides I like Matt, he reminds me of myself, only scrawnier." He glanced at Matt as he joked. Onyx rolled her eyes and continued to eat. "This man's knowledge of codes was what made him worth one billion dollars," Venom continued. "Can you imagine what an unbreakable code could do for a country's military or a terrorist group?"

"What's so special about the code?" asked Matt.

"You start with a cube, covered in numbers and letters. The cube is the cipher. Then you send quantum equations to each other. The solution to the equation is a set of coordinates that correspond to a number or letter on the cube," he explained.

After dinner we all headed off to bed. I found a women's bedroom with two bunk beds, in the dark I could just make out three figures occupying beds. I placed my bag in the corner then climbed into the empty bed as quietly as I could. Even after the nap on the plane I was exhausted. I kicked off the shoes and slept in my clothes. That night I dreamed of the man I killed. My mind replayed that moment on the yacht. I had ended a life to save a friend, but he was still dead. It was amazing how pulling a trigger like that could have such a huge consequence. He may have had a family, maybe a wife and kids. None of my training had truly prepared me for the psychological aftermath of killing. I tossed and turned in my sleep.

Red emergency lights flooded the tiny room and an alarm screeched from somewhere in the hall. In an instant I had my shoes on and bag over my shoulder. The other women were just as fast at getting their things together. We all rushed out into the hall and followed the flood of operatives through the compound and into the garage. A man in a business suit was standing on a chair shouting orders and breaking people up into teams.

"...and Martin you're on Alpha team, take two vans and leave now. Your handler will give you the details. Venom, Onyx, Matt, Holly, Dart, and Arrow you're on team Beta. Take a vest and helmet, one gunman and one driver per motorcycle. Gunmen get submachine guns. Your handlers will walk you through it all, go. You five over there, you're Delta team..." he ordered. I looked over to see two ex-military men nod to the orders, evidently they were Dart and Arrow. I rushed to a pile of gear and equipment. I donned a Kevlar vest and motorcycle helmet with a tinted visor. I picked a Heckler and Koch MP5 out of a row and another operative slapped a "Police" sign across my back. Groups of agents armed to the teeth riding though the streets would have drawn too much attention. Pretending to be a swat team we could pass by civilians without the real police being called. I slung my go bag over my shoulder. Matt straddled a bike and I climbed on behind him. In a pack, team Beta rode up the lift together and into the city.

Tonya was wired into my helmet's headset and began to brief me as soon as we exited the lift. "Your mission is to free a fellow agent who got caught by the police ten minutes ago. He is being transported by two officers to the police station. You will work as a team to box the cruiser in and hold the officers at gun point while Arrow gets the agent out. You must keep them from pulling a gun or calling for backup. When the agent is out, the cruiser is free to go and everyone will scatter. Do you understand your orders?"

"Yes," I answered simply. I didn't like the idea of going against the cops but I could never leave another agent behind or in trouble like that. My adrenaline was pumping and my heart was beating like the blades of a helicopter.

I hung onto Matt and we raced through traffic and back alleys. His handler was giving him turn by turn directions and his set of orders. Venom and Onyx were just ahead of us and Dart and Arrow were just behind us. We turned onto a main road and spotted the blue and red flashing lights up ahead. One of the black vans was stopped across the road blocking traffic, a plume of smoke spilled out from under the hood. The cruiser turned down a side street to go around and we followed. The second van rushed out of an alleyway and blocked the cruiser's path. Matt and I pulled up on the left, I raised my MP5 and pointed it at the driver. Onyx and Venom did the same on the right side and Dart blocked the rear.

"Don't move! Hands on the wheel! Don't move!" I yelled. My heart was racing, I hated seeing the fear in the poor man's eyes. His job was to stop criminals, but I knew sometimes the job required us to break the law.

"Drop the weapon and put your hands on the dashboard!" ordered Onyx.

Arrow ran up to the right passenger door and broke the glass with the side of what looked like a hydraulic bolt cutter. It easily cut through the bars on the windows.

"Hands on the wheel!" I shouted again. The driver's hand had shifted towards the radio.

In one quick move Arrow reached in and hauled the handcuffed agent out of the cruiser through the window then dragged him back to a newly arrived car. They climbed inside and the car took off. At once the van and all the motorcycles drove off in a different direction. The cruiser pursued the van and I could hear the sirens fading in the distance. I clung to Matt as Tonya gave me the next piece of the mission.

"You're off to a safe house outside the city. You're going to have to lay low and keep off the radio, the police will be scanning for us. I will call you with the next part in a few hours," she said, then added "Good job, Holly, that could have gotten messy," and with a small click she disconnected. I could faintly hear Matt's headset as Tonya continued to give him directions. The rush of the wind and the roar of the engine made it impossible to make out what they were saying. Matt slowed down and used alleys to sneak out of the city.

It dawned on me that I still didn't even know what state we were in, much less what city. He swung us around and opened the throttle as we raced up the on-ramp onto a highway. It was a risky move, we needed to put distance between us and the city, but any state patrol would be combing the highways searching for us. I looked back as we drove on and saw a sign stating that the next exit lead to Phoenix, Arizona. That explained why it was so hot in the morning, and why I was just fine in jeans and jacket over a vest at night.

After about twenty minutes we took an exit to a small residential area. Matt navigated his way to a small one-story house tucked back behind a row of tall hedges. We left the bike next to the garage under a tarp. I wordlessly raised the MP5 and stacked up on the door into the garage and waited for Matt. When he didn't follow suit I turned to look at him. He stared back at me with wide eyes as his hand hovered over an empty holster. His gun was gone. I instantly ran through the places we had been and people who could have taken it in my head. I gestured backwards, silently asking if we should go back for it. He shook his head and motioned on, we still had to clear the safe house. I passed him the MP5 and drew my Glock 2k12. We stood on either side of the door and I turned the knob and threw it open. The garage was dark and mostly empty, containing only a few gardening tools and a can of gas. We crossed in unison and opened the next door into the laundry room. Together we went room to room till we had scoured the whole house. Satisfied that we were alone I started to search for the hidden safe. Matt followed behind me.

"Should we call it in? Losing a gun is a big deal. I never wiped it down, my fingerprints are all over it," he worried.

I pulled the cushion off the couch to look for hidden compartments, there was nothing there. "My handler ordered radio silence. They will call with an update, we can tell them then." I pulled the rug back and found nothing but hardwood flooring. "We need to lay low, eat, sleep, get a work-out in, that sort of thing," I explained.

"The stash is probably in the master bedroom in the bed," he commented as he watched me hunt for it.

"You think? I would have put it by the back door for quick escape," I replied.

"The bedroom window is big enough to fit through," he pointed out.

"Alright then let's see who finds it first. You look in the bedroom and I will check out here," I said with a hint of a smile.

"You're on." He disappeared into the hall. I continued to hunt for the stash.

My phone buzzed, it was Tonya.

"Tonya, we have a problem," I told her before she could get a word in.

"I'll say. Is Matt next to you?" she asked in a rush.

"No, he is in the other room. Do you want me to call him over?" I asked worried.

"No, don't. They just found the Phoenix Director dead in his office, Matt's gun next to him. You have a traitor in your midst. Your orders are simple. Kill him and come back to the compound," she said with a forceful, compassionless tone.

"What! No, that's not possible, he would never- he couldn't have. He is my partner.... I won't," I spluttered, completely shocked.

"Holly, listen to me. Keep your voice down. We have video of Matt walking away from the Director's office, he was killed with Matt's gun. You don't have to be a rocket scientist to put that one together. We all know how loyal you are, you have risked your life over and over for the Organization. You did so today when you saved your fellow agent from the police. But you have a decision to make. The Organization has always taken care of you. Partners come and go. It's us or him. If you choose us you will be promoted, you're ready for the next level. If you choose him, you will be killed too. Come on, Holly, I know you. This isn't even a tough call," she said. I felt numb. I couldn't catch my breath. My heart felt like it was being ripped in two. I wanted so much to be a legendary agent like my mother. That had always been my dream.

Matt came out of the bedroom and saw me holding the phone. The look on his face turned from confusion to horror as a tear ran down my cheek.

"You are right, it is an easy choice," I told her as I hung up and placed the phone on the counter. For better or for worse, my mind was made up. I drew my Glock, closed my eyes and squeezed the trigger.

Chapter 12

The phone shattered into hundreds of tiny pieces. Fear, confusion, and anger threatened to overwhelm me. I pushed it all down till I could think clearly. My scalp and fingertips tingled with adrenaline. I ended up feeling emotionless and full of explosive energy. I had a plan. I could make it all work.

"Are you insane!" yelled Matt incredulous.

"Did you find the stash?" I asked in a scary calm voice.

"What the hell is going on?" he demanded.

I grabbed both of our go bags off the floor and pushed passed him to the bedroom. The mattress was pushed up against the wall leaving the steel safe exposed in the center of the bed frame. I set the bags down and found an electrical outlet. Digging in my fingernails I was able to pry it off the wall. In the hollow next to the wires was a small silver key. Matt followed me in as I unlocked the safe and started blindly filling the bags with everything inside.

"Holly!" he grabbed me by the arm and turned me to face him. "Talk to me!"

"Do you trust me? " I asked, still in the same dead voice.

"Damn it, Holly, tell me-" he started, but I cut him off.

"Do. You. Trust. Me." I asked forcefully.

"Yes but-" he answered, again I didn't let him finish. We didn't have time.

"I will tell you everything, but not now. Toss your phone and fill the bags. We have to leave, right now," I said all in one breath.

I plucked a burner phone out of the safe and got on the web. I was very much aware that the Organization was watching the phone. I found what I was looking for and kept scrolling to throw them off. Then I called a taxi to take us to the airport then broke the phone under my heel. Matt tossed me my bag and I slung it over my shoulders.

I ran outside to the motorcycle with Matt just behind me. I pulled on a helmet and held my hand out for the keys.

"I am driving," I informed him.

"I take it we aren't waiting for the taxi," he commented.

"Not if we can help it," I said. With that, he dropped the keys in my open hand and pulled on the other helmet. I drove down the road, the opposite way from where we came. Matt tapped me on the shoulder.

"This is a dead end!" he called over the sound of the motor.

"Not for long," I replied with a mischievous grin.

I revved the engine and cut though somebody's back yard. Thankfully they had no fence and I was able to drive straight though onto the next road. We sped through the neighborhood and back onto the main road. I was keeping an eye on the speedometer and was scanning for cops. Adrenaline had completely flooded my system making me hyper aware and a little paranoid. Working our way though the outskirts of the city I found my destination. A small private airport. Only problem was it was a cargo-only shipping company. On the other hand that meant it had significantly less security than a normal airport. I parked the bike and ditched the helmet. Matt followed my lead and caught onto the plan.

It was late evening, but there was still a lot of activity in the airport. We snuck to the chain link fence, and knelt down to retrieve bolt cutters from our bags. We made quick work of the fence and carefully timed our next move. When the staff member turned his back we ran to the hanger, avoiding cameras as we went. I crept to the hanger door and used a tiny mirror to look inside the hangar. The first thing I noticed was that it was dark and silent. There was a small plane parked inside surrounded by other equipment. There was a tiny office in the back with a light on but no one was inside. Together, we sprinted to the office and pulled the door open. It was a security office filled with monitors and computers. There was an open file on the desk with the current date on it. I rifled through the file as Matt looked over the security feeds. I found a list of outgoing flights for that evening and looked up the one we wanted. I spotted a cell phone on the desk and quickly pocketed it.

Without warning, Matt pushed me down and dropped to the ground next to me. He had his finger to his lips. I could hear the sound of work boots coming towards us. He army-crawled to the door and crouched next to a file cabinet. I rolled under the desk and held my breath. From my vantage point on the ground I could see the door swing open and black boots shuffle into the office. He sat at the desk and started moving papers around. His legs were just inches away from me. It dawned on me that he was looking for his phone. I saw Matt edge towards the guard, ready to take him out. I caught his eye and shook my head, telling him to wait. Silently Matt edged back behind the cabinet. The guard swore under his breath and stood up. My pulse quickened. He shuffled back out of the office and shut the door.

In a rush I let out my breath. We waited a few minutes, then stepped out of our hiding spots. Together we looked over the security feeds and found our target, a plane two hangers down. Matt took lead as we left the hanger. Sticking to the shadows we wove our way past guards and workers alike. We came to the right hanger but instead of going in we crept around back and I stopped at the fuse box. I knelt down and fished around in my backpack for a block of C4 and a remote detonator. I used my switchblade to cut a small strip from the block. Not enough explosives to hurt anyone but enough to take out the inside of the box. I passed it to Matt who placed it in the box as I zipped up my bag.

From the security cameras we knew where there was only one camera in the hanger and at least two workers loading the plane. We also knew that there was a back door that the camera only had a partial view. With the C4 in place we moved on to the back door. Matt tried the door and found it locked. I dropped to the ground and used the tiny mirror to check for anyone standing next to the door. I gave Matt the all clear, and he picked the lock. In unison we slipped in and took cover behind a pile of crates. Matt eased the door closed behind us. I checked the time, we had 20 minutes left. I wanted to use the mirror again to look around the corner but the workers might have seen a glint of light reflecting off it. I peeked around the edge of the crate and spotted the workers. I ducked back and signaled to Matt where they were, and that one had headphones on. I pulled out a radio transmitter. Matt drew the pistol he got from the safe house.

Our eyes met for a second, then I triggered the detonator. The hanger was plunged into darkness and the workers yelled in surprise. Flashlights clicked on and one worker rushed out the main door. Matt and I sprinted out towards the remaining man. He had a radio in his hand and was about to call it in. I ripped it from his hand, as Matt pistol whipped him on side of the head. I caught the unconscious man before he hit the ground, and silently laid him down. As an afterthought I grabbed a can of oil and set it on the floor on its side. I dragged the man's foot through it, making it look like he knocked it over in the dark and slipped, knocking himself out.

Matt and I tucked ourselves behind some boxes in the cargo hull of the plane and waited. After a few minutes a group of workers came back along with the security guard. We heard them talk about the incident and we were relieved when they decided it was just a power surge shorting out the fuse box. The unconscious man was taken to the hospital and our plane was cleared for takeoff. I started to breathe easier when we made it to the runway.

"Ok, Holly, spill it. What is going on?" Matt asked in a whisper.

"Your missing gun was found. It was used to assassinate the Phoenix Director. Tonya called me and said you're a traitor to the Organization." Matt started to protest, outraged by the news, but I cut him off. "Keep your voice down. I know you were framed. She gave me two options, either kill you and get promoted, or refuse to kill you and get marked for death myself," I explained, still in the same emotionless, icy tone.

"Clearly, you chose the second option," he said, still trying to process everything.

"No, I chose option three," I answered, as the plane took off.

Chapter 13

"I have a plan," I assured Matt.

"Oh, so there is a plan. I was under the impression we were simply running for our lives from the biggest, most connected intelligence group on the continent, hell, maybe the world." He ranted sarcastically.

I rolled my eyes at his lack of confidence. "We are going to land in Quebec in a few hours, then we will find Audrey. She can give us access to the Organization's forger. We can pay him or her to make us a new set of passports and we'll pay extra to keep it off record. Then we go to Paris and find my mom's stash, her real stash. Then we'll figure out what to do from there," I explained.

"What stash?" he asked confused. I dug around in my pocket and passed him the bullet notes. He read through them, and handed them back. He let out a low whistle. "Your mother was one creative agent. I wonder what it is".

"Whatever it is, I am hoping it will even the odds," I continued.

Getting off the plane was much easier than getting on. I had expected the workers to unload immediately. Instead, they left the cargo for the morning and shut the airport down. After that it was just a matter of slipping past the night guard, avoiding the security cameras and sensors. As soon as we hit the street we started looking for a place to sleep. Matt spotted a shady looking motel. We agreed they were likely to let two teenage kids stay overnight without asking too many questions, as long as we had cash.

The lobby stunk of bleach and cigarette smoke. I passed Matt a stack of $20s from my bag. Unfortunately we didn't have any Canadian money and paying in US currency would mark us as Americans. It was a risk we were just going to have to take. The man behind the counter had long greasy hair and didn't look shocked to see kids walking in the door in the middle of the night. We paid for one night and gave him a fake name. The man shuffled down the hall to show us our room. He handed Matt the key outside our room and smirked at my eagerness to get inside.

I dropped my bag on the bed, almost afraid to touch anything. The place was filthy, but it was all we had. Matt frowned at the queen sized bed.

"Crap, I forgot to tell him two beds," Matt said.

I shrugged, it was the least of our problems. "I'm going to shower," I announced.

"From the looks of this place, you might want to shower after you sleep," Matt commented.

"I will probably shower then too." I went into the bathroom with a change of clothes and closed the door.

Grabbing the bar of soap next to the sink, I scrubbed the bathtub, mostly to give myself something to do. I could feel my emotional wall starting to crack. I needed a way to release the pressure or the 'dam' would break and I could make a fatal mistake. After the tub was clean I climbed in and let the hot water try to wash away the last few hours. I couldn't stop my mind from racing. How did everything get so messed up, so fast? I had no idea how Matt and I were going to live though this. All my training and knowledge about the Organization was telling me that we were as good as dead. My one ambition, my one dream was shattered. I would never be an agent like my mother. I would never again see Nick or Dimitri, worse than that, they would believe that we were traitors to the Organization. They would think we had betrayed them. My wall crumbed, unleashing all the fear, anger and pain. I cried. The sound of the running water was just loud enough to cover the sound of my sobs. I was grateful for that at least. I didn't want Matt to see or hear me cry. When I had finished, I toweled off and dressed. I felt so much better, I had done all the grieving I needed and could now focus on surviving.

When I came out of the bathroom I found Matt already fast asleep.

I collapsed beside him, suddenly too tired to bother with the covers. I slipped into a nightmare.

I was back on the yacht, on the roof of the bridge, reliving the moment when Matt was nearly killed. This time freezing rain came down in sheets. I looked down and saw Matt stagger through the door to the lower decks with an injured Notch. Behind him a large figure wriggled silently out of an access hatch and drew his gun. I lowered my stance and pulled my own gun. I lined up the shot. I exhaled and squeezed the trigger. I heard the suppressed bang of the silenced gun, but the mercenary was unharmed. The dud bullet fell to the ground. The mercenary crept closer to Matt. In a panic I squeezed the trigger again and again. Two more duds fell to the ground. In slow motion I watched the mercenary take his stance, executioner style. It was too late to warn Matt of the danger behind him, he wouldn't have time to react. In desperation I let off one more round, the bullet left the chamber and flew though the cold salty air, right into the center of the mercenary's forehead. I blew out the breath I had been holding and slumped onto the roof. My hands felt sticky and wet. I looked down to see them soaked with blood. I tried to wash it off in the puddle on the roof that had collected from the rain. The puddle turned red but my hands were still covered with blood. I climbed down to the swim platform of the yacht and dipped my hands in the water below. I watched in horror as the whole ocean turned red, but the blood still wouldn't come off.

I jerked awake, it was still dark and Matt slept soundly beside me. I didn't need a PhD in psychology to know the nightmare was from guilt over taking a life. Killing someone is not something you can just brush off, but I didn't regret saving Matt. I knew it was stupid, but I couldn't help looking at my hands in the dark. I breathed a sigh of relief and laced my fingers with Matt's in the dark. With his hand in mine, I was finally able to fall back asleep.

The next day I watched Matt closely, I knew I had more time to process the situation. I also let off some steam, he still hadn't. We left most of our stuff in the room, hidden as best we could in a hurry, taking only our hand guns and cash. We needed to change our look and pick up supplies. There was a shopping center nearby. It took us only an hour to get new clothes, disposable phones, hair dye and a few other things. Matt grabbed some cleaning supplies from an unattended cleaning cart and stuffed them in our bag. Back in our room, we dyed our hair in the bathroom. We had been taught to change the cut, color, and texture of our hair, to hide our identity. I knew that it was what they expected us to do, but they taught it to us because it works. I chose black hair dye because, combined with the brown contact lenses, I would have the most common color of eyes and hair in the world. Matt simply went a few shades darker. I used my knife to cut my hair to shoulder length, then scrunched it with gel we just bought. Matt used a razor to cut his hair. It took us just minutes to wipe the room down with bleach to cover our tracks. Satisfied with our new looks we packed up our stuff and left. We didn't bother to check out.

Matt hailed a taxi and I gave the driver Audrey's address, hoping she hadn't heard the news yet. It was just past noon when we pulled up to a brick apartment complex. I got the address of the apartment building from Ryan's computer, but I didn't know which apartment she was in. Matt and I came up with a rough plan.

Matt paid the driver and I shrugged out of my jacket, even though it was cold out. I couldn't help look over my shoulder as we entered the building. My emotional flood was over, but the paranoia was only just beginning. The lobby was mostly empty, containing a few chairs and a fake potted plant in the corner. A middle-aged woman stepped out of a side door carrying a basket of laundry and pressed the elevator button.

"Excuse me, Miss?" I called out. She turned and looked at me curiously. "I was hoping that you could help me. A red-headed girl left this jacket at my party last night, I never caught her name but my friend thinks she lives here," I lied, showing her my jacket.

"You must mean Bailey, she lives on the third floor, number 15. That is so sweet of you to return her coat," she replied with a smile.

We thanked her and stepped into the elevator with her. She got off on the second floor and we continued onto the next level. Apartment number 15 was at the end of the hall. Matt knocked but there was no answer. After a second or too I dug out my lock picking set and prayed that it wasn't booby-trapped. The lock was simple enough, it clicked open and we slipped inside. We still didn't know for sure if it was Audrey's apartment, naturally she would use a fake name in the building to keep her home a secret. Everyone needs a safe place to run to, it was just one more thing that Matt and I lost. We spread out and searched for a go bag. It would have to be somewhere near the door and easily accessible. Matt found it in the coat closet in a few seconds.

"Well, we know she lives here, we don't know when she will be back," Matt pointed out.

I looked at the clock on the wall. "She should be at school now, then she'll have a few hours to sleep and do homework before she leaves to work with her trainer," I said.

"So now we wait," Matt said, opening the refrigerator.

We didn't have to wait long, about a half an hour later we heard the scraping of a key in the lock. I took cover by the front door and Matt stood around the corner into the kitchen, just in case it wasn't Audrey. In unison we drew our guns and held our breath. The door handle turned and slowly inched open. Audrey crept into the apartment with her gun drawn. My hand shot out and pulled her gun from her grip. She took a swing at my head and I dodged.

"Audrey, chill out, it's me!" I yelled at her, backing away.

She paused, a look of realization appeared on her face. "Holly? What are you doing here? My neighbor told me someone was looking for me and I thought…" She trailed off, turning to look at Matt, who had just stepped out from around the corner.

"Hey Audrey, long time no see," he said. He had already holstered his gun.

I handed her back her gun and put mine away. "We need your help. We are on our first assignment, but lost our fake passports and need new ones. It was a stupid mistake and we don't want to report it. Matt and I were hoping you could tell us where the Organization's forger is."

"Oh, that's right, you two are agents now, congrats. Umm…. I can get you the address," Audrey said as she walked over to her computer and booted it up. She opened a file and started looking though names. "I know the guy, I had to pick up a package from him a few weeks ago." She found the right file and wrote a number on a sticky note.

"Thanks, you've really saved our skins, Audrey," Matt said as we gathered our stuff to leave.

"Happy to help, good luck with whatever it is," she wished us.

Back on the street, we found another taxi and gave it the address on the note. I tasted blood and realized that I was biting my lip out of anxiety. After about a 45-minute ride, the taxi stopped outside of a used bookstore. I swung my bag across my back and followed Matt into the store. Matt let the door close and switched the "open" sign to "closed".

I marched up to the man behind the counter. "We would like to place a rush order," I informed him.

"Sure, ID number?" he asked getting out a pen and paper.

"Put it under 96648361." I gave him Audrey's. She was helping us out more than she knew.

He typed the number into the computer behind the counter. I held my breath hoping that Audrey's picture wouldn't be displayed. "Certainly. Always a pleasure to work with the Organization. How many items will you need?"

"Six, three for each of us." I told him.

"Which countries do you want?" he asked setting up a camera and backdrop.

"France, Russia and England." Matt told him.

"Do you want each one to have a slightly different picture, different clothes, hair cut and etcetera?"

"Yes," Matt answered.

He took our pictures and up-loaded them to his computer. "Your total comes out to about one mill".

"Perfect, when will they be ready?" Matt asked.

"Tomorrow around noon is the best I can do," he said.

Matt and I left the store and walked to a new motel, thankfully a slightly nicer one. We got a room and ordered room service. We planned our next move as we ate overpriced soup and sandwiches. Our money was running out fast, we still needed to buy plane tickets to Paris. We would have to ditch our guns and weapons to get though airport security, everything but my mother's gun and locket. I was sad to part with the switchblade, I had had it for so long, but there was no way to take it with me.

It had been a whole day on the run from the Organization and we weren't dead yet. Perhaps, we were better than we thought. Or maybe they were just biding their time. The motel had a gym so we decided to workout to pass the time. Even on the run we've got to keep in shape.

The next morning we packed all of our things into two bags, one that we could get though security with, and one we had to dump. I emptied my gun of bullets and taped it to my inner thigh. I then pulled baggy sweatpants on over it. The high-tempered plastic gun itself could pass through a metal detector, I just had to make it past the security.

Matt wiped the room down while I got maps and information from the front desk. We checked out by 10:00 AM, and walked eight blocks or so with both bags.

Finding a place to leave the guns was tricky. A dumpster would be too sloppy and found quickly, we weren't close to any body of water, and we didn't have time to break into an abandoned apartment or business. We settled on a manhole because it was convenient and would likely be left alone for months. We dumped the bag containing all items that airports generally frown on, like guns, duct tape and bolt cutters, in a manhole, then found a small café for brunch. After eating we walked the rest of the way to the used bookstore. There was a old couple looking over books when we got there, so we pretended to do the same until they purchased a few novels and left. The clerk put a manila envelope on the counter as we put the books back on the shelf.

"All six items, as promised. I must say they turned out flawlessly, especially for a rush job," he commented.

Matt opened the envelope and looked them over.

"I trust you want me to just bill your friends. You know, you two are by far my youngest customers," he continued curiously.

"Pleasure doing business with you," I said, ignoring his age comment. Matt replaced the passports and closed the envelope.

With that, we left, called another taxi and directed it to the Quebec City Jean Lesage International Airport. I counted our cash, then took a few bills from the bag and put them in my pocket. We had enough money to get two tickets. I had no idea what we would have done if we didn't.

The taxi dropped us off in front of the entrance. I paid the man and we shuffled inside. I pretended to be admiring the ceiling-to-floor window as I scanned for security and tails. I looked over the different airline ticket counters. I picked a name at random and stepped into line. When we got up to the front of the line I asked if they had a flight to Paris for that day. To my luck she said they did and I purchased two tickets for nine hundred each, leaving us with just a fistful of cash and what I had in my pocket. I tried to act as confident as I could, despite the woman's suspicious look as I handed her the large stack of U.S. dollars. For a second I thought she was going to call security, but she looked at the long line of people behind me and handed me the two boarding passes. Declining her offer to check our only bag, we hurried off. I checked our flight time, we had an hour to kill. Buying the ticket was the easy part, getting though security with fake passports and a gun would be the hard part.

Stepping into the line for security check, I began to slow my breathing and mentally recite the times table. Praying to no one in particular that Matt and I looked like the average tourist with a lot on our mind, we produced the tickets and a pair of passports. The security guard scanned them, then waved us through. We stepped into a second line and removed our shoes and jackets. Under the watchful gaze of two guards and dozens of cameras, we placed all of our belongings into plastic trays and slid them along a conveyer belt to a x-ray scanner. I knew my gun wouldn't set off the metal detector, but that didn't mean the trained security wouldn't spot my nervousness or the gun itself. I slowed my breathing down too much, I tried to stifle a yawn, one of the guards asked me if I was sleep deprived. I told them with a small, polite smile that I just needed some coffee. I refused to think about what would happen if they found the gun. Matt stepped through the scanner first without incident and started putting on his shoes. I wanted to hold my breath and close my eyes when the guard waved for me to step through, but I forced my body to stay relaxed and my breathing regular. I forced myself to look bored and stepped through.

Chapter 14

The scanner didn't go off. I gathered my things and walked with Matt a few paces away to slip my shoes back on. Slowly, I let my breathing come back to normal. We walked off to find the right gate and get a bite to eat before our flight. Passing an overpriced bookstore I saw a little girl clinging to her mother's hand. Before I knew it I was lost in a memory.

I was five again, walking with my mother on our way to the park. I held her hand tightly as we walked. These outings were rare and made my mother anxious, in turn making me as well. At the park I played on the jungle-gym equipment as my mother watched from a bench. After a half an hour, a man walked by, dropping a thick envelope on her lap. She stood up and called me over. Hand in hand, we walked back towards our apartment. When we reached our street she pulled up short, picked me up and sped off in another direction. Over her shoulder I saw what had scared her. Two black vans were parked out front and men in dark coats showed something to one of our neighbors. The envelope turned out to contain a large stack of foreign currency. We stopped at a bank to retrieve two passports from a safety deposit box. I saw my mother drop an envelope in the passport's place before we left. I expressed my concern for my toys and possessions, as we took a train out of the county. She told me that we weren't coming back, which was a shame because I liked France.

The hour passed uneventfully and so did the nearly 9 hour flight. It felt weird to be sitting in another plane so soon, but this time we got a bathroom and actual seats. I heard people complain about having to ride business class and I wanted to tell them to try a cargo plane sometime. I

95

tried to pass the time by planning our next move, but after a half hour I realized I was getting nowhere. I closed my eyes and took a nap.

After what felt like a blink of the eye, I woke up as the plane started to descend. Again, my head was on Matt's shoulder and his arm was around my waist. I sat there for a moment, feeling safe for the first time in a long time. I finally sat up and stretched.

"First, Hawaii, now Paris. These past few days could almost pass for a vacation. Traveling was one of the reasons I joined, but I never thought I would see it like this..." Matt trailed off.

I knew exactly how he felt. I had imagined traveling the world on exotic and dangerous missions too, although I always imagined the Organization would be on our side.

"Beautiful view," Matt commented.

I glanced out the tiny window at Paris shining in the dark. "It is," I replied.

"I wasn't talking about the window," he said quietly, gazing at me. I blushed a little.

We left the Charles de Gaulle Airport without incident and hailed a cab. Before climbing in I did a quick perimeter check to scan for anyone following us. I gave the driver an address. Matt shot me a confused look. He was expecting the address from the bullet code, this address was totally new. I laid my head on his shoulder so we could whisper.

"Where are we going?" he asked.

"Do you remember when Nick gave us a break to change for sparring, back in Hawaii? I used it to talk Ryan into letting me use his laptop. It wasn't easy either, I had to bribe him. I took several Organization safe houses offline and erased all record of them. I memorized their address and info," I explained.

"Bribed him with what?" he asked shocked.

I rolled my eyes. He wasn't upset that I had kept a secret from him, he was jealous of what I might have done to convince Ryan to help me. "I gave him a chocolate bar that I found in the kitchen," I said with a faint smile. Making Matt jealous was a novel form of entertainment. I scanned the other cars again.

"Americans, yes?" asked the driver in a thick French accent. Matt's accent was obvious even when he wasn't speaking English having learned all his foreign languages in his teens. I, on the other hand, had not only been exposed to different languages growing up with my mother, but I also began studying them when I joined the boarding school at age 6.

"Oui et non, il est americain. Je suis Canadien," I lied. It was better for him to think that only one of us was American. Two American travelers would better fit what the Organization would be looking for.

"I give you tour, show you Paris!" exclaimed the driver. I knew it was a scam. He would drive in circles, costing us a much bigger fare.

"Non," I started to decline as I glanced over my shoulder again. I spotted something that made me change my mind. "Oui, Oui, si vous plait".

Matt looked at me with concern, sensing that I was tense. I used hand signals to tell him that a car was following us five cars back.

There are several different ways to check if you are being tailed. The most common is to take a complicated series of turns, and watch to see if you are the only one making them. This is the method I used to ID the black sedan five cars behind us. However, it can be thwarted if the tail is working with a team, each taking turns to follow. The fastest and most dangerous method is to simply stop in traffic, forcing the tail to either do the same to avoid losing you or move on and let you go. This too, can be thwarted with a team. The most effective, and my personal favorite, is to force the tail into an environment that they can't camouflage. Once out in the open you can take more aggressive action, not just ID them or lose them. All of these work on foot as they do in a car.

I whispered in Matt's ear, "How do you want to play it?"

He whispered back, "We need them on foot, take away their cover." He raised his voice to address the driver, "We change our minds, we want to party!' The only problem was we weren't dressed to go clubbing and had no idea if we could get in.

"I know good place," he said, turning the car sharply. The tailing car was forced to turn also. If I wasn't sure we were being followed before, I was then.

I stuffed a few bills into the driver's hand the second he pulled to the curb, we were out of the car before he had time to stop. I turned the duffle bag so it was in front of me with the zipper facing in so no one could pick-pocket from it.

It was late, I had no idea how late, and we were in front of some teen night club. The bass was audible even through the heavy steel doors. I stuffed the last of our cash into the bouncer's hand and pushed through. Inside was darker than on the street. The black was punctuated by neon strobe lights. I could feel the bass in my chest. The club was so crowded we had to hold hands to keep from being separated. We pushed through the throng of dancing drunks and made our way to a booth in the back. I used the table as cover to move my gun from my thigh to my waistband. Not that anyone could have seen me in the dark corner anyway. Matt sat on the back of the booth to see over the tops of people's heads, searching for anyone that stood out. Matt and I were extremely young for agents so anyone from the Organization would be older than this crowd. A girl in an impossibly tight dress stumbled out of a tiny hallway next to our booth. I poked my head around the corner to see. There were three doors, two were labeled as bathrooms and the third an exit. I quickly started formulating a plan. Matt was still scanning when I yelled into his ear to be heard over the music. He nodded his agreement. I left the duffle bag with him and went to the bar. While the bartender was busy I grabbed a piece of paper, a pen, and a strip of tape. I returned to the hall and taped the paper to the men's bathroom and wrote "en panne" to keep anyone from entering without raising suspicions.

Next I ducked under the table at our booth and changed my top and jacket. Matt kept watch on the door as I worked my way back to the front door. As I walked, I put my hair into a ponytail. It still felt strange to have such short hair after cutting it in Canada. I found a spot to stand by the front door. We didn't have to wait long, about a minute later the door opened and two middle aged men pushed the bouncer to the side and entered. They split up and scanned the crowd. Matt's head ducked down and I stepped further into the shadows. The first guy passed within a foot of me. He put his hand on his holstered gun. My pulse quickened as I saw what he had clipped to his belt next to the gun. It was a full syringe.

Generally I hate night clubs, bars and strip clubs. It's not my idea of a great way to spend my time. They usually don't smell great and never play my kind of music. But as far as being followed by middle age operatives carrying guns and nasty-looking syringes goes, we couldn't have been in a better place to take them down.

I stepped behind the first guy, practically invisible with the music, lights and crowd. I pulled the syringe from his belt and injected him in the neck as fast as I could. He grabbed my wrist in surprise and froze for a second. I caught him as his feet went out from under him. It was difficult to look normal as I dragged the unconscious man across the room and sat him in an empty chair. In seconds I had searched his pockets and taken his gun. I made a beeline for the remaining guy who was working his way to Matt. Staying just a few paces behind him I checked the new gun, it was a Glock, fully loaded. Matt stood up and made eye contact with the operatives and walked into the bathroom with the "out of order" sign. Naturally the operative unholstered his gun and followed. I melted into the crowd as he scanned for me before entering. I followed with his partner's gun out.

As I entered the bathroom, I was greeted by the sight of the operative backing Matt into a corner with his gun pointed at his heart. I raised the stolen gun and pressed it into the small of the operative's back. He froze.

"Placez-le sur le sol, lentement," I ordered. He hesitated. I cocked the gun to convince him I meant business. I stepped a pace back, out of arms reach as he placed the gun on the filthy floor, like he was told.

"Bonne. Parlez-vous anglais?" I asked him. Mostly for Matt's sake, my French was fine.

"Yes," he replied with a slight tremor in his voice.

"Kick the gun over to my friend and don't get any ideas. I promise you I won't miss at this range." He quickly complied. Matt picked it up and checked it. Then, addressed the operative; "You get three strikes, then the janitor gets a nasty surprise in the morning. Answer every question quickly and without lying. Try anything and a bullet goes in your knee."

Rather than acting shocked or intimidated, the operative looked in disbelief from Matt to me. "You're Organization, too?" He must have recognized the basic approved interrogation script. "Zut, your young. Wait, why is there a hit out on our own?" he asked.

I lowered my gun and didn't let my guard down. Matt explained, "I have been falsely accused of killing a Director."

"You? No way. It's all over your body language. I bet you've never killed. Ice princess over there looked like she still might put a round in me. Even then, they are supposed to send a Retirement Agent, not me."

Ice princess? He gave me too much credit for my acting. Or did he? Honestly, I would put a round in him if he tried to kill Matt, or myself. It no longer mattered to me that he was an operative, he was a threat. I didn't hate him, I envied him a little.

"What were your orders?" asked Matt.

"A bunch of operatives have been taking shifts watching airports and train stations in their off hours, looking for two teens. I wasn't even sure it was you until she did the perimeter check, and I knew you weren't civilian." I mentally cursed myself for being too conspicuous.

"Why don't we strike a deal?" I said. The operative turned his attention back to me. "We are on the same team here. Neither one of us wants to kill the other. We could simply leave like nothing happened, you and your partner forget this ever happened, report a false alarm."

The operative mulled it over. "Okay, but only because I never signed up to kill kids. You will still have a Retirement Agent after you," he warned. I lowered my gun, relieved.

I threw him a cocky smile. "We can handle it. You don't mind us keeping your guns, right?" I turned to leave with Matt close behind me.

Just before I opened the door and went back to the crushing sound of the club music I hear him mutter, "You know, you remind me of someone I used to know."

We ducked out the back door and though to a dark side street.

"Where to now?" Matt asked, tucking his new gun into his waistband for lack of holster.

"The first safe house I took offline is in the red-light district, and we need cash, supplies, not to mention sleep." I looked around the side road and at a street sign across the road. "Crap, I think we're lost." I retraced our path in my head and imagined a map of Paris. We left from the Charles de Gaulle Airport and headed west for 30 minutes. Looking around, it seemed likely that we were somewhere in the red-light district already. I scanned the rooftops for the Moulin Rouge's signature red windmill lighting up the dark sky, but only saw apartments above clubs and small businesses. "Okay," I waved my hand around, indicating the side road, " this is point 'A', point 'B' is the safe house, how do we connect two dots?"

Matt thought for a second. "We also need cover or protection to prevent that little incident from happening again, or at least so soon," he said. "Maybe find a drug dealer that could lead us to someone worth making friends with, like a money launderer, gang leader or drug lord. They could also point us in the direction of the safe house."

I smiled at his solution. "I like it, let's go find a drug dealer".

Slowly and carefully we made our way further west, dodging cameras and bystanders as we went. Our tiny side street let out onto a main road with two rows of trees lining a walkway between them. There was light car and foot traffic, we tried to blend in with the latter. We passed bars, clubs and cafes along with a few shadier businesses. The closer we got to the Moulin Rouge the heavier the foot traffic got as it shut down for the night. Matt spotted a man loitering around in the walkway lined with trees. In a heartbeat, Matt and I assumed our unspoken roles. He griped my upper arm and dragged me along. I shuffled and shivered despite the moderate weather, wiping my nose and sniffling. We were the picture of a jonesing addict and her controlling boyfriend. The man wandering around spotted us and made a beeline for us.

"Elle regarde comme de la merde, j'ai quelque chose qui va la réparer". He commented on my condition and offered something to help.

"Montrez-moi," Matt demanded in his best French. The dealer complained and flashed a plastic bag of white powder. I sighed longingly looking at it. "Pas ici, il est trop ouvert," Matt said looking around. The dealer lead the way to a more private spot. We crossed right in front of the Moulin Rouge and walked through the glow of its red lights. On the dealer's heel, we stepped into a tiny alleyway.

Calling over his shoulder, the dealer warned us that the drugs weren't cheap. As one we drew our guns. The startled dealer pleaded and offered the drugs for free. Matt patted him down and emptied the contents of his pockets onto the pavement. He had a cell phone, twenty Euro and several bags of drugs. Not being an expert I could only speculate on what kind. My best guess was heroin, mainly because that is what the French Corsican mafia deals. Also, I faked heroin withdraw symptoms and the dealer would have known what different drug withdrawals looked like and pointed me to someone who had what I wanted, if he didn't have the drugs.

He had several bags and very little cash. I used the phone to check the time, it was a little past 2am. I didn't know what kind of business hours this dealer kept, but I assumed he was nearing the end of his night.

Either he had a slow night or was planning on making one big sale.

I addressed the dealer in French and asked if he had a bad night or a big customer. He whimpered. I just barely kept from rolling my eyes, some street hardened criminal he was. I backed off some but didn't let my guard down. He told us again that we could take everything he had. I ignored the offer and asked him again if he was going to meet someone. He said that he was going to sell to an escort. Matt chimed in and said that it was a lot of heroin for one hooker. The dealer explained that she was the middle man and was going to take it to one of her clients. Matt asked where he was going to meet the girl. The terrified dealer said he was to meet her right in that alley, any minute now. I told him he had 5 seconds to tell us everything he knew about her. Most of the intel was useless but we did find out that her name was Charlotte. She was exclusively seeing an arms dealer named Chase Moreau, who sometimes lost his temper and beat her. Charlotte never uses, but the arms dealer went through a lot of heroin.

I thanked him for the information and told him it was his lucky day. I took his phone and bag of heroin and told him we were going to let him live. Matt and I sidestepped so he had a clear path out of the alleyway and ordered him to get lost. The second he was gone I handed the drugs to Matt and went back to the walkway outside to wait for Charlotte. I checked the time on the phone, it was 3 a.m.

We didn't have to wait long. A gorgeous woman walked our way in a red tight dress and heels that must have cost a small fortune. She ducked down the alleyway and I followed. She froze when she saw Matt in the dealer's place.

She gave Matt a dazzling smile "désolé, mon erreur. Je pense que je suis perdu," she said, turning to leave.

Matt replied, showing her that he had the drugs. "J'ai le produit, si vous voulez toujours".

I stepped to block the alleyway. She moved to step around me, still wearing the same smile. I blocked her path again. Her smile disappeared. I asked her if she spoke English.

"I no want trouble," she said in a scared voice.

"Who blacked your eye?" Matt asked.

"Nobody, I fall," she said, looking back at him.

"Did Chase hit you?" he asked gently.

"You know about him?" she asked wide-eyed.

Matt gave her a small, friendly smile. "My friend and I solve problems. You seem to have a big one. If he hits you, why don't you leave him?" he asked.

A look of helplessness came over her. "He.... He has passport. I just want to go home. I go to Paris to study, but I want to go home."

Matt and I looked at each other, I nodded. Our plan had changed but only slightly.

"We will make you a deal," I offered. "You get the drugs and get to keep your money. You come with us to a safe house where you write down everything you know about Mr. Moreau in exchange for a new passport." The intel she could provide would give us an angle on the arm dealer who could in turn provide short term protection and weapons if we needed more than what was at the safe house.

"New passport? How?" Charlotte asked, amazed.

"There is a passport making kit at the safe house," I told her.

"Do we have a deal?" I asked.

"....Oui, we have deal," she said. I saw a spark of hope in her eyes. It's what made her agree, despite her gut screaming at her to run.

"Do you have a car?" asked Matt.

"um... Oui," she said surprised by the turn of conversation. "Block over".

Matt tossed her the bag. "Let's go."

The three of us filed out and found her car. I decided that Charlotte was an okay person, you know, for a girl who sells herself for cash and extremely nice shoes. But in my line of work, who am I to judge? I gave her the address of the safe house. We were closer to it than we thought, it took us only ten minutes to get there. Matt and I swept the tiny one bedroom apartment while Charlotte waited in the hall. Once satisfied that each room was clear, we checked the two windows, one in the living room facing the main road and the second in the bedroom facing a side street, both were covered by blinds. Matt found the stash first, four black duffle bags in the washer and dryer's lower drawer. Matt and I laid it all out on the bed and Charlotte looked on in a state of incredulity. I picked up the passport kit and turned to Matt.

"Do you want to do it or do you want me to?" I asked.

He kept sorting equipment and clothes, discarding what we

couldn't use or transport. "You did better at the forging seminar then me, you should do it," he pointed out. I nodded and handed him the bag from the previous safe house.

Charlotte followed me back to the living room. I sat on the couch and opened the plastic case, spreading things out on the coffee table. I picked up the Polaroid camera and looked through it.

"You will need a different shirt for your passport picture," I informed Charlotte.

"This one should fit her," Matt said tossing a blue t-shirt to Charlotte. "You can change in the bathroom." Charlotte returned wearing the blue shirt and resumed watching me work.

"What country do you want to be from?" I asked her, holding up an assortment of passport covers.

"Switzerland," she said looking at her options. "Have anything to eat?"

I pointed at the kitchen. "Knock yourself out." I realized how hungry I was. Matt and I hadn't eaten or slept since the plane.

I picked out an ID page that matched Charlotte's description. I called her back to take her picture. While it was developing I stitched the pages into the cover. When the picture was ready I cut it out with a box cutter from the kit and glued it into the precut indent on the page. Charlotte wandered back from the kitchen eating yogurt with a spoon.

"I figured out, you guys are CIA, yes? I mean, you're American, with safe house, you make passport, want to know about arms man. I am right, aren't I?" she asked.

"Yup" I answered, deciding to run with the theory on the fly. "Your passport is done." She went to grab it but I pulled it back. "Info first," I told her. I placed a note pad from the kit in front of her with a pen.

I cleaned up the rest of the kit and added it to the equipment pile in the bedroom. Matt was still sorting so I raided the kitchen. I grabbed two containers of yogurt and spoons. I returned to the bedroom, gave Matt one of each and sat cross legged on the bed among what I assumed was the weapons we were keeping. From my spot I could see Charlotte through the open door. I finished my yogurt in five huge spoonfuls. Matt dumped a bag of burner phones in my lap so I could pick one. I selected a small, simple phone and dumped the rest in the discard pile. We didn't say anything, not because we were mad or worried about

Charlotte overhearing anything, but because we didn't need words to be on the same page. I strapped on a Kevlar vest under my jacket before I pulled two backpacks from the clutter, one for each of us. I divided the clothes that we bought in Quebec and folded them tightly. Matt already had his vest on and handed me a toiletries kit for each backpack. I put the clothes and kits to the side so I could pack them last, that way the top layer of the backpacks had normal contents. I picked up a box of ammo and refilled my mother's gun. Matt handed me two MAC10s with suppressors and extended mags. I checked the safety and ammo and packed them in the bottom. I added a med kit, lock picks, extra ammo, extra holsters, packaged food, duct tape, our 6 passports and all the cash Matt had found to the packs. Matt ran his hand over a sniper rifle in its case but left it. I found a shoulder holster and strapped in my mother's gun. I was picking through the remaining equipment looking for a switchblade when Matt handed me a hunting knife, my hand lingered on his as I took it. It wasn't elegant but it would work. Zipping it into an outside pocket I finished packing the bags.

"Done," announced Charlotte. I passed Matt her passport along with the empty yogurt container and spoon. He left the room as I started repacking the discarded equipment back into the duffle bags.

Matt read over her notes and nodded. "Congratulation..." he paused to read the passport, "Anna Holms, you are the proud owner of a brand new passport. Next step, pack your things and head home." He traded her for the notes and sat next to her on the couch to finish his yogurt.

I gathered the duffle bags and headed to the laundry room. As I passed Matt a loud ringing came from one of the bags. Matt jumped to his feet, followed by Charlotte. I dropped the bags and dug out the ringing cell phone. I didn't recognize the number but that didn't mean anything. Pressing the call button I held it up to my ear.

"Holly, did you think you could just disappear?" My blood ran cold at the sound of Tonya's voice. "Last chance, put a bullet in him and you get to walk away".

"He is innocent. I'd rather die than kill him," I told her. Matt pulled a extra MAC10 from the bag, catching the drift of the conversation.

"I am sorry to hear that, I had so hoped you would change your mind. You were a big investment, you know. You could have been great, maybe greater than your mother." She was baiting me. "Oh, and Holly...," she added.

"What?" I asked in an venomous voice.

"That jacket is not flattering," she taunted. I could hear the smile in her voice. I dropped the phone and hit the ground. Matt followed my lead. Charlotte's head whipped back with the sound of breaking glass.

Chapter 15

Matt and I were in the bedroom before her body hit the ground. We scooped up our backpacks and slung them on as more bullets tore the apartment to pieces. Instinct kicked in as I flung myself out the window. I oriented myself in the air and combat-rolled as I hit the ground two stories below. The impact knocked the wind out of me, but I scrambled to my feet as Matt landed behind me, MAC10 in hand. Bullets whizzed past, coming from the building across from the safe house. We sprinted into traffic, dodging cars as we went, and headed for the heart of Paris. Matt stuffed the gun under his sweatshirt as we ran. Generally speaking, running for your life while carrying an automatic weapon tends to catch the attention of cops. We kept running, putting as much distance between us and the unknown number of operatives.

Maybe the agent from the club was right, perhaps the Retirement Agent had caught up to us. Or maybe the agent hadn't kept quiet and lead a team to take us out himself. Or perhaps Ryan hadn't kept my activity on his computer quiet and the Organization had been staking out all the safe houses. Either way, they had found the safe house I took offline, making all the other safe houses, ironically, unsafe. I analyzed the shooter to figure out who was after us. The way that my conversation with Tonya was timed with the first shot made it clear that she and the shooter where commutating with each other, meaning they were on the Organization's payroll. The speed that Charlotte was taken out meant that the shooter was already targeting her when they were given the order. Charlotte being targeted and not Matt or I was strange. Perhaps the shooter was using thermal imaging to see us through the walls, which could explain the mistake. The fact that shots were only fired from one spot meant one shooter. The lack of resistance in the side street meant that he didn't have backup or a partner and couldn't pack up his rifle in time to pursue us. I shoved all this out of my mind for the moment to focus on surviving the next few minutes. We needed to get off the streets, and lay low. Hopefully the address in the bullet code was a safe house that the Organization didn't know about.

There was little traffic now that the city was sleeping. Without foot traffic we couldn't blend in. We were burning adrenaline and would crash soon. Suddenly a thought popped into my head that made me slide to a standstill. Matt shot past me and had to skid to a stop before standing next to me. I pulled the cell phone from his pocket and threw it on top of a bus passing by, hoping that it would keep them off our trail. Matt didn't ask any questions so I guessed he knew what I was thinking: if the Organization knows to call one phone in the set they could easily track the one phone no longer sitting in the safe house. My eyes swept the streets as we went, looking for cover, watching for cops or operatives, trying to avoid cameras.

Distance is a little hard to judge when sprinting through an unfamiliar city, but I think we went three miles before we slowed down to a steady run. We ran another two or three when a street sign caught my eye. I made a quick turn to dart down a different street with Matt a step behind me. I slowed my pace as I scanned the buildings. Running to a door, tried the knob and found it was locked. I pulled the lock picks from my bag and set to work. I couldn't believe our luck, we had stumbled onto my mother's safe house by accident. Once inside the apartment lobby, we locked the door behind us and crept up the stairs looking for the right door. We finally found it on the fourth floor. I pressed my ear to the door to listen for a moment before picking the lock. Inside was pitch black, except the entry which was illuminated by the hall light, and it smelled like dust. Something bothered me about the rug on the floor but I couldn't place it right away. I caught Matt's hand and pulled him back before he set foot inside. On a hunch, I knelt down and pulled back the corner of the rug, underneath was metal contact plate and wires. I whipped the rest of the rug off to reveal the path of the wires. They traveled up the wall and into an outlet. We stepped over the trap and inside, closing and locking and the door behind us. With our small arms drawn we cleared the one room apartment in seconds. Once sure there were no more traps we flicked the lights on and collapsed, exhausted onto the couch.

Matt turned to me curiously. "What kind of trap was that?"

"A fire trap, judging by the way it was wired into the outlet. The outlet is likely rigged to ignite flammable material in the walls," I answered closing my eyes.

"How did you know it was there?" he asked, fluffing up a dusty pillow.

"My mother always told me never step on the first rug in every rental house and apartment we ever had. I thought it was so it wouldn't get dirty, but then I wondered if it was something more," I replied with a yawn, curling up on the old, but surprisingly comfortable couch.

He might have said more, but I was already asleep. Overwhelmed by exhaustion, I was dead to the world. My mind was just as tired as my body and no dreams came that night.

I awoke on the couch, curled into a ball. Matt sprawled across two thirds of the couch, still asleep. My stomach growled, reminding me how hungry I was. Easing myself off the couch so as not to disturb Matt, I unfurled and stretched. I took a minute to take a serious look at the apartment. There were windows blacked out with newspaper and aluminum foil. That, coupled with the fire trap meant we had the right place. The only furniture that the apartment had was the couch, a table, two chairs and an end table with a lamp. In the corner there was a washing machine. It took me about 5 minutes to quietly go through all the cabinets and the refrigerator, finding only dust. The clock on the stove said it was 6 a.m. I decided to go to the tiny grocery store we passed on our way to the apartment. Thinking that either we would starve if we just hunkered in or I would get shot like Charlotte while out, neither option scared me. The detached way I regarded my chances of dying unnerved me. I told myself to think of my goal. Stay alive and find a way to prove Matt's innocence, failing that, simply keep Matt alive as long as I could. The thought of my death didn't faze me, but the thought of his death was unbearable. I forced myself to clear my mind and get dressed to leave. I couldn't find paper so I left Matt a note on a piece of paper towel on the little table in the center of the room.

With my hair hidden by the hood of my jacket and a little cash in my pocket, I left the apartment and crept outside. I tried to keep my head down, act normal and watch everything all at the same time. The traffic on the road was light and the foot traffic was lighter. Once inside the store I glanced about to map out the exits and surveillance cameras. Growing up in the Organization, I learned to eat healthy and cook simply, there were better things to do with my time than explore the culinary arts. I gathered fruit, vegetables, lean chicken, yogurt, eggs and pasta. I made minimal eye contact with the store clerk as I handed her the large denomination bill. All of the cash from the safe house was in large denominations to transport the maximum amount of money with minimal bulk. The clerk checked it for counterfeit before giving me the change. I was back on the street ten minutes later, and after checking for a tail, I was at the apartment door in another five minutes.

I had just barely stepped over the fire trap when Matt crushed me and the groceries in a bear hug.

"Where the hell have you been, I thought you were dead, or hurt, or changed your mind," he said in a breathless panic.

I wiggled a hand free, covered his mouth, and reminded him that we couldn't let the other residents know that we were there. Once he had calmed down I explained that I had gone to get food and had left a note, which he had overlooked in his panic. When his breathing had finally reached normal I left his side and went to the kitchenette. I fried two eggs and poured two glasses of water. Matt set the table, still a little tense. I couldn't get a read on him, I didn't know if he was embarrassed by his panic attack or just lost in thought.

After breakfast, Matt searched for my mother's stash while I did laundry. The apartment held a outdated washer but no dryer. I hand washed our cloths in the sink with the laundry detergent I found tucked next to the washing machine to avoid any unnecessary noise. Hiding out in an outdated apartment in Montreuil, washing jeans by hand, oh yeah, I was living the dream. I cut the blinds cord from the window and strung it up in the shower in the bathroom to dry the clothes. Matt had searched the street side of the apartment, disassembling the nonessential pieces of furniture to look for a hidden stash. With the laundry done, I joined him in the search. After two hours we still hadn't found anything and had covered the entire apartment several times over. We took a break and ate some of the fruit from the market.

110

"The stash could be hidden in an infinite number of places," he said, showing his frustration.

"Not infinite, it's within these walls and it has to be hidden somewhere hard to get to if it was going to stay hidden for a decade," I pointed out. He didn't seem too encouraged.

I went back to the search while Matt cleaned the guns, even though they hadn't been fired yet and didn't need it. Mostly he needed something else to do for a bit. I was just starting pulling the broken air conditioner out of the wall, when Matt started laughing while holding my Glock. I tried to hush him but he didn't seem to hear. His eyes were fixed on the table in front of him.

"You know, I could just end it, I am dead anyway. At least this way it's my choice. It's the perfect solution. Just tell them you did it, you would be back in and this mess would be over."

I was by his side in a heartbeat. I slid the gun from his hands and pulled out the mag before setting it down. I was worried but also a little relieved. I had expected Matt to break down ever since I got the call in Arizona. At least I didn't have to wait any longer.

I spoke gently but firmly. "Look at me, Matt. It's been three days. They couldn't touch us in Canada. They tried to kill us twice in one day and we are still standing here without a scratch. We have plenty of money, weapons and we are safe now. We will find the stash and clear out. I can fix this." Matt had no way of knowing that my pep talk was just as much for me as it was for him. With my reckless attitude that morning it was clear the stress was getting to us.

He finally looked up at me. "Why are you here Holly, why didn't you "fix this" back in The States or in the last safe house? I heard Tonya offer you a way out again." The look in his eyes was impossible to read.

"I... I don't know," I said, taken aback by the question.

"Bull shit. You know exactly why, but you can't let anyone into your heart or your head. Maybe growing up a killer-to-be means that you will never let anyone in, but you can't sit there and tell me you don't know. I cared about you since I met you three years ago. I thought that in time you would work through whatever your emotional baggage is, and figure it out."

"I could never kill you. I would rather die, hunted down by the Organization, then hurt you."

"Then let me in. No more secrets."

"My name is Hanna King. My name is written in Arabic on the necklace she left for me. I think I was born in London, my mother wasn't big on talking about the past. I do know that we lived in thirteen different countries before I was six. She was killed in our apartment in Russia and the Organization took me in. I studied at the Boarding School for four years before graduating from recruit to trainee. Nick became my trainer and we toured Europe. I was enrolled in different schools to learn how to blend in different countries and social classes, but trained to be an agent at night. At eleven we moved to North America and did the same in Canada and the U.S. At thirteen we met and trained together for three years, you know the rest," I told him. It was more than I had ever told anyone.

"What about your father?" he asked quietly, after a moment.

"I don't know, my mother never said anything about him. We never needed him." I told him truthfully.

Matt's body language changed, his shoulders slumped and he looked up into my eyes.

"Do you think we are going to make it?" he asked.

"I don't know for sure, but I do know we are going to give them hell," I answered.

A new possibility occurred to me. The Organization might want whatever was in the stash and was simply letting us do the ground work for them, throwing in a few bullets and operatives to turn up the heat to insure that we worked quickly. It would explained how two young agents seemed to stay ahead of the entire Organization, and the Retirement Agent, who still had yet to make an appearance. If it was true, things were going to get very interesting the minute we had whatever my mother hid.

With that thought, I laced my fingers with Matt's and had a second epiphany of the afternoon. It was no accident that Matt and I were paired. The Organization knew how to create a flawless team, with each one's strengths compensating for the other's weakness. I remembered Nick's words to us when we first began to train together. "Your partner is your most valuable asset in the field. Your partner keeps you going, keeps you sane, keeps you strong and keeps you fighting, long after you thought you couldn't go another step." Back then, I had no idea how true his words were.

I kissed him on the cheek and I went back to the air conditioner as Matt cleaned up the guns, replacing them in the bags and holsters. When he had finished he started to work out. He could only do so much in the limited space and needing to stay as quiet as possible. I pried the back panel off and removed some wires and hoses. I blinked in astonishment as I stared at a small safe, carefully fitted in to the hollowed out air conditioner. That explained why it was so heavy, and why it didn't work. I made a small sound of relief.

"Finally," Matt said, smiling as he looked over my shoulder.

I looked at the digital key pad and screen, counting seven spaces for numbers to be entered. I shuffled numbers and letters in my head for a second before punching in 8114141. I had the safe open in less than five seconds. Pulling the tiny door open I gazed at my true inheritance.

Chapter 16

I blinked down at a thick stack of files topped with one white envelope. I grabbed all of it and shoved it into my backpack. Swinging it onto my back I stood up and examined the apartment.

"How did you know the code?" asked Matt incredulously.

"I guessed. I knew it was something seven digits long and had to be something she knew I would guess. She told me the answer when she left me this." I held up the locket. "The answer is my name. It's a simple conversion, a number corresponds with a letter of the alphabet. H(8) A(1)N(14)N(14)A(1), giving you the number 8114141," I explained.

Matt grinned, "Spy is in your blood."

I grinned back and changed the subject. "Now that we've got it, we should clear out, get moving again. We can look it over later," I subjected.

Matt looked at me, surprised. "Aren't you dying to know what's in it?"

"Yes, but I have a feeling that if we stick around for much longer, we will be dying for real," I told him.

It took us a few minutes to wipe down the apartment and destroy all evidence of our presence. Leaving the apartment from the back exit we made our way to the closest bus stop. We could have taken a taxi, but to leave less of a record we chose to take a bus. I remembered passing a bus stop on my way back from the market. It was less than 50 meters away. Perfect for a quick getaway... but bad if we needed to hang around waiting for a bus. At the bus stop I looked up the bus schedule and routes while Matt kept an eye out.

At last the bus showed, running ten minutes late. We both grabbed aisle seats and scanned the crowd. The majority of riders were on their way to work or out shopping, but the group of six North African teenage girls were clearly hell raising. I had heard of France's "girl gangs" but I didn't expect to run into them in Montreuil. I thought they would be further north in the poorer neighborhoods. Unlike the more traditional gangs, these girl gangs dabbled in things like mugging, beating up rivals, pick-pocketing white tourists and generally being loud and obnoxious.

As a teen age white girl traveling with what they would assume was a boyfriend, I knew I was a likely target for harassment and pick-pocketing. I pulled my hood up and tucked my hands into my pockets to hid the color of my skin. The human eye is particularly attracted to movement and bright colors. Matt and I wore browns, blacks, and grays to blend in, but I was careful to match the movements of others around me, effectively become invisible in plain sight.

I used the window's reflection to watch the girls as they clapped, chanted and tried to be intimidating. Using hand signals I told Matt that I thought they could be a threat. He acknowledged and studied our surroundings for other threats.

The bus stopped and we stepped off with a small crowd, listening to the girl gang to see if they were following. The bus door slid shut, cutting off the girl's songs behind them. One threat gone, hundreds left. As I spotted the Gare de Lyon train station just ahead, I noticed a man following us as we made our way to the ticket booth. He was in his late 50's wearing a business suit and holding a large briefcase. There was nothing alarming about an older business man taking the train. But in the evening, and a weekend – Not exactly rush hour. Families, honeymooners and elderly couples made up the majority of the people around us. Also, I couldn't be sure from a distance but it looked like his jacket had a similar cut to the ones that the Organization issued, designed to conceal a weapon. Fear and my training sent me into a state of controlled paranoia. I was watching everyone and everything. Classifying them as either a threat or not, not a simple task as the Gare de Lyon is one of the busiest terminals in Europe.

At the ticket booth, Matt and I showed a different set of passports then the ones we used to enter France. We bought tickets to Florence, Italy, with a connection through Milan. We bought first class tickets, expensive but we would have our own sleeper car, in theory a safer ride.

If we had booked a sleeper car shared with two or four others we would have needed to sleep in shifts. We needed to be fully rested to stay one step ahead of the Organization and their Retirement Agent. We grabbed our tickets and made our way to the right terminal. I lost sight of the business man, he must not have been following us after all.

We had a little time to kill before our train departed, so we bought a newspaper at a kiosk. Seating ourselves at a small table against a wall with a decent escape route we looked over what my mother had left for me. We started with the letter on top.

To my beloved Daughter,

Congratulations in making it this far, I am more proud of you than you will ever know. But this is not the end of your journey. The information enclosed will lead you to the one man in the world that can answer your questions. You deserve to know the truth about me, your father and the Organization.

Getting to this man won't be easy, but nothing worth having ever is. He will know who you are and that you are coming. Luckily for you, he wants to talk to you almost as much as you want to talk to him.

Call my contact, his information is listed, and use his code name that I have left for you. He will give you all you need to get to the Founder of the Organization.

Lastly I pray you don't let yourself get consumed by the lies and politics of the Organization. I hope you find happiness and love. Perhaps you will even find a way out of the Organization all together.

I love you with all my heart, never forget that.

-Alison King

I whispered to Matt, "that's our ticket out, the Founder." The noise in the terminal was loud, but we still didn't want to take any chances. I thumbed through the intelligence files. "This must be how we find him."

"Looks like you are going to get your answers about her and your father after all," he pointed out.

"I don't really care about my father, I just want one answer. Who framed you and why?" I told him.

"What about her name?" he asked.

"Alison King? I don't know, I have never seen that name before," I replied.

"Don't you know your own mother's name?" he whispered.

"Not her birth name, I always called her mom. Her name changed with every new passport and every new country," I explained. "In the Organization I just knew her as Bridget, legendary agent."

"She gave you her real name. You could find out who she was before the Organization. You could have family, relatives out there somewhere," he whispered, excitedly.

My mind crushed the spark of hope in my heart. "They destroy all records of someone when they join. It's not like we could just Google her and find her life's story. Besides, happy children from happy, well adjusted families don't become agents. The Organization recruits orphans with no one left to miss them. Look at you and me."

Putting the rest back in the backpack, we boarded the train with the other travelers. Once on, we found our compartment and did a security sweep. I waited until the train had left the station before I pulled the files back out. I laid all the pages out and started trying to make sense of it all. Like all intelligence files it all looked like unrelated people, places and data. One by one the pieces fit together, each a puzzle piece that matched an aspect of another document. After a full two hours we stood back and looked at it as a whole. There was one, seemingly unrelated page with her contact's information on it. The rest was detailed research on a man's life. We assumed he was the Founder. He lived on a yacht, a comfort to us as we had already worked an op on a yacht. She had found a pattern in his seemingly random pattern of travel. There were also detailed profiles and the ports he stops at, the people who travel with him and the yacht itself. It looked like years of work to gather all this information.

"She must have been planning an operation, but it went bad. Leaving her out in the cold and you to pick up the job at least a decade later," Matt commented.

"But if she was legendary, why would she plan something against the Founder? If she was that far in, why go against the Organization? Did she get framed, like you? Why frame someone so valuable?" I thought out loud. My mind was spinning with questions. I was hoping her stash would answer my questions. Now, if I wanted the answers I would have to do what my mother said and get to the Founder.

I turned my attention to the contact's information. I read the code name across the top and my heart skipped a beat. Samson. My mother's contact was just as legendary as she was. But he was her contact ten years ago, we didn't know if he became her contact before or after he left the Organization. If he really was out in the cold, we didn't even know if he was still alive or if he would help us. The info my mother left for us had to be outdated, someone as elusive as Samson would have to stay on the move and leave no record of his whereabouts. I didn't even know if it was possible to find someone who was hunted by the Organization while we were being hunted ourselves.

It was too much to process at once. I had to step away or my mind would just keep spinning. We packed all the files back into the backpacks and took them with us to the dining car. Matt and I ate in silence, both lost in thought. Our table was at the center of the car. Matt sat facing one half and I watched the other half, literally watching each other's backs. We finished our food quickly, without really tasting anything.

It only took about half an hour before we were walking back to our compartment. I saw out of the corner of my eye a face I recognized, but when I turned to look I just saw a door closing. I thought it was the business man I had seen back at the station, but I wasn't sure. It was possible that he was just a simple traveler, maybe my paranoia was getting out of hand. Once back in our car I whispered my suspicions to Matt and rechecked the room for bugs and cameras.

"What threat level do you think he is?" Matt asked after we were sure nothing had been touched in our absence.

"No idea, he could be a Retirement Agent or just a civilian," I told him. If it turned out to be nothing I didn't want Matt thinking I was losing it, then again I was taught that the one thing I don't tell my partner will be the one thing that kills them.

"Then we will be careful, but manage that threat when it comes to it," he said. I agreed.

We pulled the files back out and I went back to sorting and analyzing it all. Ordinarily I would just snap a picture of everything and send it all to an Organization analyst. Being out in the cold was a serious strain on all of our abilities. Matt and I were both trained in reading intelligence files, but we just didn't have the experience or the recourses of the nerds that used to be one phone call away. I used the back of a sheet to take notes and draw out the pattern. It looked like the Founder's yacht should be in any number of ports in Italy or Greece, but there was still a chance he was not following this decade-old pattern. The yacht had a strange name, The Cicolluis. I dug through the piles of paper till I found a half sheet with the same name handwritten across the top. It said Cicolluis was a Celtic god of war, their version of the Greek god Ares or the Roman Mars. The second line on the page said the name Bridget was derived from the Celtic Goddess Brigantia. Under that line there was a question: Connection? It looked like my mother was still looking into some of this when she died. It was odd that a code name and the name of the Founder's yacht was from the same obscure mythology. I wondered which came first. I swapped papers with Matt who was looking over the security notes of the yacht and its blueprints. From the handwritten notes in the margins, it looked like Bridget couldn't find a way of being invited onto the yacht or have an excuse to be on it. There was no way of sneaking on during the day or while it was traveling. Leading a covert mission when it had laid anchor at night was the only possibility. She highlighted tiny holes in their security and weakness' in the staff.

I turned to Matt and rubbed my eyes. "Ok, we need a plan, any ideas?" I asked.

"We need to check the listed ports in Italy, then move on to Greece. Oh, and staying alive might help," he said with a grin.

"Why don't we get a burner phone and try Samson's contact info? It's a long shot but it wouldn't hurt to try," I suggested. I gathered up most of the files and sat on the bed, lost in a new train of thought. Making a decision, I turned to Matt and said what was on my mind. "No secrets, right? I can ask you anything?"

"Anything," he answered curiously.

I took a deep breath before asking, not sure if I wanted the answer. "Why did you join the Organization? You told me about your mom's death and that they gave you something to fight for, but what was it?"

He looked stunned by my question for a second. "Well, you were honest with me, now it's my turn. The operative in the club was wrong, we both have killed."

My eyes flew to his face with surprise, but he just looked at the floor and continued. "The Organization found me after my mom was killed by that drunk driver and offered me revenge. They told me he was out on bail. They gave me a gun, a name, an address. They showed up right after

I did it and told me they would clean up, only they didn't. They even planted more evidence against me. The police started hunting me and the Organization made me an offer. I could go to prison for first degree murder, or join them and disappear." His fists where clenched and his knuckles where white. I slid off the bed and walked over to him. Winding my fingers with his, I uncurled his fists and held them. He looked into my face. "Why do you want back in? All they do is ruin lives. We could fake our death and just disappear, you and me. We would be free," Matt said softly.

"I think my mom tried that already, and look what happened to her," I pointed out.

"We don't know that, we only have part of the story," he countered.

"The only way to stop them from hunting us is to get back in. My mother had a plan, let's see how it plays out. It worked so far," I said.

"Fine, we could always fake our death later, if we don't die for real," Matt said.

"That's the spirit," I said with a grin.

We packed the files away, locked the door and slept. The next morning we woke early to make the train connection from Milan to Florence. Packing everything into the backpacks except for the Kevlar vests under our large jackets, we made our way to the dining car for breakfast. I kept an eye out for the business man. I saw him exit in a crowd a few cars over, but lost him after a minute. Matt and I bought three burner phones at a kiosk. We talked it over for a minute and decided that the train station was the best place to call Sampson's contact number. If our call was traced they wouldn't know where we were heading. We found a quiet corner and Matt dialed the number. We held our breath while it rang.

It rang for a long moment before going to a generic voicemail. Matt left a message. "Mr. Samson, I was given your number by a mutual friend, Bridget. I have a situation that could use your expertise. I have lost funding from the company and really need your help to get the job done. Hope to hear from you soon." He disconnected the line with a click and turned the phone over to pull out the battery and SIM card.

We boarded without incident and I still watched for the business man, but didn't see him. Other than being afraid for our lives, riding across Europe was pleasant. The second train ride lasted only a few hours. It didn't give us enough time or privacy to get the files out again, so we passed the time quietly mapping out the order in which we would check out various ports. It would have been easier to check the ports by going into an internet café and looking on satellite imaging maps, but those can be years out of date and wouldn't show us if The Cicolluis was in that port currently.

I still hadn't seen the business man again and decided that I had been paranoid. The kind of fear that comes with being hunted by a huge unstoppable group of killers tends to make you a little irrational. I reminded myself to keep watching my surroundings, but not think that everyone in a suit was out to kill me. The train pulled into the station and we left the car in a crowd of other passengers. Matt and I followed the flow of people towards the exit when something in my peripheral vision made me turn around. It was the business man walking in the same flow of foot traffic towards us. He was carrying a folded newspaper with both hands and his face was blank, but something was off. As he got closer I saw the end of a silencer covered by the newspaper. My hand flew to my Glock. I took it off safety and turned on the active camouflage. Our eyes met. I stepped in front of Matt and took a bullet to the chest and one to the side.

Chapter 17

Matt spun around as I hit the ground. I couldn't breathe. The business man started to disappear into the crowd, who still hadn't figured out that shots were fired. I drew my Glock and returned fired. I didn't have a clean shot at his head so I put a round in his knee. He hit the ground with a gasp as Matt grabbed the top loop of my backpack, dragging me away. The crowd started to panic and scream. My eyes scanned the people pushing in around us, looking for any possible threat. The business man might have backup. My adrenaline was maxed out as I tried to breathe and look at everything at once. Matt hauled me onto my feet and with my arm around his shoulders, hurried me out with the scared pedestrians. I stuffed my Glock back in its holster, flicking the safety back on and active camo off. My breath was coming back in ragged gasps. I started walking on my own and dropped my arm from Matt's shoulders. We ducked our heads as security ran past. Outside, Matt pulled me to the side, away from the crowd.

He forced me on to a bench. "Where are you hit?" he asked. Matt looked me over and tried to use a tone of practiced calm, but it was also mixed with urgency and a little panic.

"I'm fine, he hit the Kevlar. Just knocked the wind out of me, that's all," I told him pealing the two bullets off the body armor under my shirt. One was right over my heart, the other had hit me in the side.

"You're not hurt?" he asked still with a look of worry on his face.

"No, I'm good. He didn't even crack a rib," I explained.

His expression changed from worry to anger. "In that case, what the hell where you thinking?" he demanded, grabbing my upper arm and dragging me away from the station.

I pulled my arm away but continued to walk with him. " What do you mean?" I asked him.

"What would possess you to step in front of me like that?" he said outraged.

"I guess I wasn't thinking," I deflected.

"Shocker," he said sarcastically.

"I'm sorry, would you have rather I used you as a human shield?" I asked just as sarcastically.

"What if he had been aiming for your head?" he asked, not looking at me. We hurried away from the station. We could hear sirens.

"Well, if he had been aiming for my head and I hadn't moved, we would both be dead and we wouldn't be having this conversation," I said, looking for a bus or taxi.

"You're not immortal, Holly," he said.

"I never said I was. Look, I get it. You're mad you didn't see it first and save me. I'm not some damsel in distress, I can handle myself. I guess this is why partners shouldn't get this involved. Things get more complicated," I said, the last comment was mostly to myself. We kept walking, looking for a hotel. Florence was beautiful, almost more breathtaking than a shot to the chest.

"My feelings aren't going to change," he said, his anger was fading and working its way out of his system.

"I know, I am not asking you to change. You're my best friend, we have fought side by side for years. I will always want to fight for you. We just need to make it work. Tactically, we both handled it perfectly and you did save me by pulling me out," I told him.

We kept moving away from the station. Constantly looking over our shoulders and scanning for trouble. After a few minutes Matt spotted the Retirement Agent limping along further down the street behind us. We took off running, my bruised rib made it hard to breathe while sprinting but the Agent's knee would slow him down more. Often chases are less about speed and more about maneuverability; they can't follow you if they can't do what you do. My rib wasn't bad enough to prevent careful parkour.

Florence and Paris both tend to have ornate apartments with wide windowsills and decorative molding. Usually I couldn't care much about a city's architecture, but on the occasion I need to use these as handholds for climbing a building, it's nice to see the builders take time to add these touches.

Matt and I ducked down an alley. Neither of us where tall enough to reach, so I gave Matt a leg up to the first indent in the building's façade. I used his body as a ladder to climb up to the tiny ledge and further up to the first window. We free-climbed to the top of the apartments. The roof was moderately sloped and we both laid still, away from the edge as the Agent entered the alley way. The sound of the cars were loud enough, but I couldn't help holding my breath as I heard him walk cautiously down the alley. I looked at Matt and pointed along the connected rooftops back the way we came, doubling back would help throw our new friend off our trail. When we heard him move on, we carefully rose to check that he was gone before running across the roof to where it ended at the next block. The block ended in a road, not a main street, but definitely more traffic than the alley. We took the chance of drawing attention to ourselves as we quickly made our way down. I made up my mind to tell anyone who tried to stop us that we were in love and running away together to elope. Hand in hand we took off in another direction and went for several blocks before slowing down so I could catch my breath. My rib made it hard to draw a full breath.

I chanced a glance behind us and spotted the Agent limping towards us a block and a half away. It felt like my heart had stopped in my chest. It should have been impossible for him to follow us, let alone catch up to us with the state of his knee. Matt spotted him a second later, by then I already had a plan. A bus was coming our way from a cross street. Hand in hand we dashed across the street in front of the bus and ran alongside it the second it hid us from the agent. Matt and I effectively disappeared. We went a block before cutting down another street and zigzagged until I got lightheaded from lack of air. We stepped into a clothing store and slipped out the back exit.

The Retirement Agent lost the element of surprise. We now knew that he wasn't afraid of attacking in a crowd. Matt and I knew what he looked like and he was injured, but if half the stories about the Retirement Agents were true, then he would still be coming for us. We needed to put distance between us; we needed to get off the street. Matt and I wove our way through the streets trying to dodge store security cameras and exposed sections of street with no cover. Neither of us were old enough to get a rental car, another cab would be expensive, stealing a car might draw too much attention, so we agreed to try to make it on foot for at least until we had more of a plan. Matt spotted an electronics store and told me he had a new idea. We quickly made our purchase and then kept walking. It wasn't cheap, but if it worked it would be worth it.

"We need to end this game of cat and mouse, bring the fight on our terms," he said, "rather than waiting for another ambush as we blindly run for it".

"Agreed, but we need to stall, this project will take time to set up," I replied.

"So we need a safe place to crash for the night, preferably cheap," he said.

"There might be a youth hostel. Our business man wouldn't be able to blend with such a young crowd. Plus we can handle any trouble we run into at a hostel," I said.

"It wouldn't be that safe, but at least we would have a better chance at seeing him coming. We would have to sleep in shifts," he said.

We asked a local for directions and speed-walked to it, looking over our shoulder the whole time. I was out of breath again by the time we found it. Matt talked the man working there into renting us one bed because we were short on cash and planned to sleep one at a time. The man lead us to a room lined with bunk beds. He told us in broken English that the bathrooms were way down the hall. The room was at least cleaner then the motel Matt and I had found in Canada. Some of the bunks were occupied, but about half were empty. I sank on a bottom bunk and took my backpack off, Matt sat next to me. I opened my pack and carefully took out the med kit so as not to flash any of the more concerning equipment inside. I knew we couldn't show any guns here, but a blade shouldn't be too unusual as long as we were discreet. Matt started opening packages that we had bought at the electronics store and got to work wiring pieces together. I found an instant ice pack in the kit. I subtly unstrapped the side of my vest and held it to my side, a slight gasp of pain escaped my lips. Matt's head whipped up to look at me. I waved it off, to show I was fine, and looked for the food we packed. We both knew my rib would heal, but it could be a problem if I had to fight. I could feel the bruise and found it had spread the length of the rib cage, about the size of my hand splayed flat. The second shot had hit me right over the heart. It was bruised too, but not as badly.

Matt looked back at his work. "That rib must be at least cracked, you're having too much trouble breathing for just a bruise," he said under his breath.

"It's not floating, I will be fine. Maybe I will tape it in the morning." I told him in a bored sounding voice, trying not to seem as concerned as I truly was.

A teenage boy Matt's age sat down on the bed next to us. He pointed to me holding my side and spoke in quick Italian. After a moment of blank stares he saw that we didn't understand what he said.

"Your boy hurt you?" he asked me in a heavy accent, indicating Matt.

"Non, a mugging," I told him in a French accent. We were using French passports from The Forger, might as well play the part. It was also a better story than 'actually I was shot earlier today, but no big deal because I am wearing a bullet proof vest'. I passed a granola bar to Matt and opened one for myself.

"Traveling can be dangerous without someone to protect you," he replied. I could see he was really getting on Matt's nerves.

"We are fine, merci. Have a bon evening." I turned away and ate my granola bar. He hesitated for a second then returned to his bunk on the other side of the room. After eating, Matt handed me a section of the project to work on. At lights out Matt insisted I sleep first and I didn't argue with him. I handed him my pack and laid down. He sat at the end of the bed and finished the project. So far the youth hostel had been a good call. The other people there were our age, making anyone older stand out instantly and, other then the friendly Italian, no one bothered us.

I don't recommend sleeping in a bullet proof vest and gun holster. They are not terribly comfortable and with my busied side, it took me what felt like forever to fall asleep. As I slept I dreamed.

I was back in a tiny apartment with my mother. We were sitting at the table with a chess set between us. She was trying to teach me how to play, but more importantly how to think.

"Look at the pieces, each is good at something. You just have to put them in the position to do what they do best," she explained in that ever-patient voice of hers.

"But I keep losing pieces," I said, frustrated.

"The goal is to get the other person's king while keeping yours safe. Losing pieces is a part of playing the game. You have to think about what the other person might do and expect that, anticipate it." She reached across the table to cup my chin in her hand. She smoothed out the little frown on my face with her thumb. "And try to keep a poker face so your opponent can't see what you feel and guess what you're going to do."

"What's a poker face?" I asked confused.

"It's being mindful of your expressions to hide your true emotions," she told me.

"But what's poker?" I asked impatiently.

"That's the next game, you get to learn." She explained with a sweet smile and reset the board to play again.

At 2 a.m. Matt gently woke me to change watches. I traded spots with him and sat on the end of the bed with the backpacks unzipped in my lap, leaning against the wooden post of the bunk bed. It was odd to sit in the dark listening to the sound of several people breathing. It felt like I was back in the dorms of the Local Command Center or in the dorms of the Boarding School. Being in both of those places seemed like a lifetime ago. My thoughts wandered back to my dream. My mother taught me a lot of things that most kids don't learn, or at least so early. Looking back I can see that the game was so much more than just a game. She was teaching me strategy, how to anticipate and use the way I present myself to my advantage. Today I was an awful chess player but the other lessons stuck. She never got a chance to teach me poker, that I learned in the dorms of the Boarding School. Unlike chess, I was good at poker; no one, save Matt and maybe Nick or Dimitri having spent the last few years together, could read my poker face. I learned to wear it everywhere in the field.

Movement across the room snapped me out of my thoughts. One of the guys carefully got out of bed. I assumed he was off to the bathroom but I was ready, just in case. He looked at me, but my head rested against the post as I pretended to sleep. He moved to the next bunk and slowly unzipped a girl's bag. He rooted through it till he had a handful of cash and moved on to the next bed. I moved even slower than he did as I drew my hunting knife from my backpack pocket. He moved on to our bunk and slowly reach out a hand through the horizontal wooden bars of the bed to the backpacks on my lap. Like lighting I flicked open the blade and drove it into the bar, catching his long white sleeve. His hand was pinned, but not hurt. He made a tiny squeak of fright, but held perfectly still. It was the Italian.

"I think we'll keep that, if you don't mind," I whispered calmly.

"I... I.." he stuttered.

"Was just about to put the money back," I finished for him.

"My grandmother is very sick-" he pleaded but I cut him off.

"Liar." I grabbed the edge of his partly unbuttoned shirt and pulled it to expose the tattoo on his shoulder. It had faintly been showing through the shirt in the light when he first talked to me. "I have to admit, prison and gang tattoos all look rather similar to me."

"Stupid bitch" he hissed and pulled a pistol from the waistband of his jeans. "you just brought a knife to a gun fight," he smiled smuggly. "Now hand over the knife and your cash."

"Silly me, what was I thinking," I said in an unconcerned voice. I drew the Mac10 from the backpack. The poor kids eyes bulged and he tried to take a step back, forgetting that his sleeve was still caught. "Oh look, mine is bigger. Put your 9mm toy down and replace the cash you took."

"Who the hell carries a machine gun?" he asked.

"People with bigger problems than you. Now, drop the gun and give back the cash," I ordered.

He placed the gun on the ground and I pulled the knife from the wood. He crept back to the other's beds and replaced the money. His eyes never left me, nor did mine leave him. When he had finished I picked the pistol up from the ground.

"Now what?" he hissed at me.

"Now you leave, you were planning on doing it after stealing anyway, am I right?"

"My people will hunt you down and kill you!" he threatened.

"Your people? I think not. Your stealing pocket change in a dump, you're entry level or on your own. Either way you don't order people around, and I doubt you're going to tell anyone you lost to a tourist girl," I said.

He swore at me and left.

I knew I should have handled that more subtly, the last thing we needed was more attention. If we had more cash I might have been able to turn the kid into an asset, but what was done was done.

   In the morning I filled Matt in on the adventures of the past night. He acknowledged, but wasn't mad about how I handled it. I found the showers while he paid for thirty minutes computer access, looking for the perfect spot to set our trap. Before replacing the vest I used athletic tape from the Med kit to tape up my rib. It wasn't perfect but it would have to do. When I finished, I paid for our breakfast and took both dishes over to Matt. He showed me the map of the place he found, and the bus route to get there. We picked out escape routes and backup plans. We switched and I looked over the map of the area while Matt showered. With that all done we left for the bus stop, looking for the Agent the whole time. After paying for our tickets we were pretty much out of money. We rode for what felt like hours. Once we got off at our stop we walked to the warehouse we had looked up. It was a Sunday morning and they had only one guard on duty as far as we could see. He was making slow laps around the building. It was easy to slip past him, along with the exterior cameras and get up to the side door. After checking for an alarm system I kept watch as Matt quickly took out the lock pick set and opened the door. Slipping inside we again checked for guards and alarms. Finding neither, we unpacked our new equipment. Home field advantage only counts if you use it.
   I found the security office and looked over the camera angles. Like we expected, there were two blind spots, one of which we used to get inside. I searched the desk and found a roll of duct tape. I tossed it to Matt in the center of the three-story industrial shelving rows. He used it to add adhesive to the backs of three units we wired the day before. They were basically floodlight motion detectors wired to burner phones. If something set off the detector, a third phone in Matt's jacket pocket would go off. Each homemade alarm was programmed to set off a different vibration pattern. That way Matt would silently know which alarm was tripped. We placed one on the wall in the back corner of the warehouse. The other two we each placed in the blind spots after timing our move carefully with the guard's pace, which we watched from the security office. Picking hidden places that still had an unobstructed path was harder than I had expected. Once back in the warehouse, we found

pallets stacked up against the wall. We broke a few apart as quietly as we could. Carefully, we passed the boards up and placed them on top of each shelving unit. Afterwards we scouted cover, blind spots, vulnerable spots and vantage places. With that done we had a tiny lunch of whatever food we had left in the packs. Matt's phone buzzed rhythmically as the guard circled.

Its hard to just sit right before an operation, especially the ones you make up on the fly.

As we expected, the guard came inside at the end of his shift. We watched him pack up his belongings in the security room from the vantage point on top of the shelves. He chatted briefly with the night guard that came to replace him, then left. The night guard did a quick sweep of the building then took up his position outside the warehouse and started making slow laps around the building. We laid on top of the shelving until he had made his second lap.

Leaping silently to our feet, we slid the 1 x 4 slats from the pallets to bridge the tops of the shelving, tossing the roll of duct tape to each other and securing the ends of each. Most of the boards covered the third tier but a few bridged the second, only 12 feet or so off the ground. With a network of boards in place we climbed down and shifted to crates to form cover but sill look orderly. I ran the perimeter and checked blind spots for Matt's vantage spot on the third tier of the center shelf. Matt had placed his cell phone on the far shelf on a metal bracket, so every time it went off you could hear it from anywhere in the quiet warehouse. Our bags were placed next to Matt's spot and all weapons were strapped to our bodies as best we could.

With all that prep work done, I climbed back up to Matt and sat next to him. He pulled the pieces of the phone we used to call my mom's contact out of his pocket, put it back together and turned it on. If anyone was tracking the phone it would now act like a beacon. The Agent didn't make his move at the hostel, we hoped it was because it was too risky with the other teens in the room. He wasn't afraid of making a move in public but he would have had a hard time to blend in. A quiet warehouse would give him more than enough cover to do whatever he needed and the night would give him time to get his knee cleaned up.

I was almost getting bored sitting in silence next to Matt as the phone buzzed every few minutes like clockwork, when the phone missed a beat. I sat up straight and looked at Matt, eyes wide. The silence pressed in and the second buzz still didn't come. I rose to my knees. Silence. My heart was pounding, I could feel it in my fingertips. I took my Mac10 off safety, Matt nodded and did the same. If we were going to survive the night we would have to give it everything we had. That meant going lethal, after all it was self-defense.

I scrambled across the boards and down one tier. I got to my hiding spot and froze, waiting. A heartbeat later the power went out. The lights died, leaving three dim emergency lights and the two glowing exit signs. I held my breath and listened for a hint of where the Agent might be.

An explosion above us rocked the silent warehouse. A hole in the ceiling was ripped open and rubble rained down right on top of Matt's vantage point. Matt rolled off his perch, fell three stories and landed on the hard pavement. He rolled out of the fall and darted into the dark warehouse. Two black forms repelled through the hole and sent a short burst of gunfire my way. I briefly saw that they wore specialized goggles, likely night vision and, based on the perfect entry point, thermal too.

The thermal and night vision goggles would give them a huge advantage. Not only could they see perfectly in the dark, but they could see us through thin cover and could see the heat of foot prints we left as we ran. The only drawback was that the goggle would give them zero peripheral vision.

I was behind several crates but could hear their movements. The larger of the two men walked with a limp. They split up and the smaller one walked down the row, I could hear his footsteps approaching my tiny hiding spot. My heart pounded in my chest like it was trying to rip free. I must have had enough cover that he couldn't see my heat signature. He was about to cross under a board just to my right. The phone across the room buzzed, in the silence it sounded like a jack hammer. In the same instance, he spun and fired towards the sound, Matt fired his Mac10 at the space where the sensor was, and I ran to the center of the board above the new agent. The explosion of gunfire covered my footsteps, and his limited field of sight was directed at the phone. He never saw me coming. I slid off the board and hung there by my knees. I grabbed the man's head and broke his neck. Gunfire stopped, and not only from his gun. He slid to the ground and I twisted off the board, landing next to him. The sound of me falling brought more gunfire from the remaining agent across the warehouse. I returned fire from my Mac10 and sprinted up the row as boxes and crates splintered and were ripped apart. I dove down the next row and the gunfire stopped. Matt provided me with cover fire as I moved up a tier and closer to the center for a better shot. I couldn't see the Agent but flashes of muzzle fire made it easy to guess where he was taking cover. I leaned out from behind a large crate and fired on the Agent. He dodged back behind his own crate. I pulled back and army-crawled along behind crates on the far edge of the shelf. I came to another gap and fired again. My Mac started to click. I was out of ammo and didn't have another mag. He must have been out too, because I heard the metallic bouncing and then rolling of a grenade. I balled up and covered my ears and squeezed my eyes shut. I could see a flash of red through my eyelids and the sound was deafening even with my ears covered. The flash bang must have been close. I sprang to my feet and ran across the next board. A hand shot out to the shadows and grabbed my ankle and pulled. I fell hard. I pulled my mother's gun from its holster and twisted around to face the Agent. My vision was still spotty and he caught my wrist and twisted until I dropped the gun to keep my wrist from breaking. With embarrassing ease he pulled my knife from my pocket and tossed it to the ground. He pulled me into a choke hold and used me as a body shield from Matt. I clawed at his hands and arms but couldn't break the hold. He dragged me to the front of the warehouse to the large open space by the security office. I was held too tightly and too close to get any leverage and break free. He put the muzzle of his silenced pistol to my head. The lack of oxygen made my vision begin to swim and fade.

"I am done playing games with you children. Throw down your weapons or she gets it in the head," he ordered.

All was silent again for a moment. In the darkness three red dots appeared, spaced out, from atop the shelving in the center of the warehouse. I gasped for air and whispered an explanation to the Agent. "Snipers." I took another sucking breath, "didn't.... think we would.... come alone... did you?"

The Agent pulled me high till my feet barely brushed the floor. My hands and feet where going numb. I needed air.

"I can see it's just the two of you. Surrender or the girl dies," he ordered, calling our bluff.

Matt was concealed in shadow. His Mac10 clicked softly. I assume it was put on safety, and the gun fell to the ground.

I couldn't yell out to Matt, or even shake my head if he was watching. My vision was beginning to tunnel. I knew I was as good as dead either way. I prayed Matt wouldn't give up, he still had a chance of living. I knew I had to do something to give Matt the chance to run, my life was over but I could still save his. I guessed which pouch held lethal grenades. I knew the blast wouldn't reach Matt. I couldn't tell him goodbye. I reached back to find the pin.

Chapter 18

As I reached back, the silence was broken by a second explosion. The Agent stumbled back a step, but held the choke hold. The smoke across the warehouse started to clear, barely showing a man-sized hole in the wall. My oxygen-deprived brain registered a giant walking towards me. The Agent aimed his gun at the newcomer. The crack of a single, un-silenced shot rang out and I felt the rush of air as the bullet flew just inches past my face. I hit the ground and gasped for air. Shaking, I rolled over to see what had happened. The giant was still walking towards me, aiming a rifle from the hip. The Agent's hand was a bloody stump, his gun was on the ground. I clutched my throat and coughed, trying to see again.

Without missing a beat the Agent drew his combat knife with his one good hand and rushed the giant. The Agent ripped the giant's rifle out of his hands before he could reload then aim the long barrel, threw the rifle into the pile of crates and slashed at his throat. The giant dodged and trapped the Agent's wrist, broke it and let the knife fall to the ground. The giant kicked the knife out of reach, giving the Agent a split second opening to jab the giant in the face with his elbow. It connected with a crunch with the giant's face, breaking his nose. The Agent pulled back just enough to kick the giant right over the knee cap, possibly breaking it. The giant fell to one knee and released the Agent's wrist. With broken wrist and stump the Agent fished a grenade out of his tactical vest, crammed it into the mouth of the kneeling giant and pulled the pin. The Agent backpedaled for all he was worth. The giant spat the grenade into his hand and threw it to the opposite side of the warehouse.

It exploded the second before hitting the far wall. The Agent crouched and scrambled to pick up the fallen gun next to where I laid. I was still shaking uncontrollably. The giant had just stepped up behind the Agent when he finally picked the gun up. The giant planted a kick in the small of the Agent's back, knocking him to the ground. The gun fell from his hands and he struggled to get up. The giant reached down, grabbed the back of the Agent's Kevlar vest and pulled him into a kneeling position. The Agent desperately clawed at the giant's hand on his back. Reaching into his own tactical pouch, the giant pulled out a short length of det-cord. He wrapped it aground the Agent's neck and pressed the detonator in to hold it in place. With both hands the giant threw the Agent behind him, back towards the hole the giant had entered. He leaned down and grabbed my upper arm and dragged me away a few paces, with his other hand he triggered the det-cord.

For the fourth time that night an explosion rocked the warehouse, the flash lit it up for a second. I cringed, and tore my arm away from the giant. I fell next to where the Agent's gun had landed after being knocked from his hand. I turned over and grasped the gun, aiming it at the newcomer. He reached down and grabbed my wrist, pointing the gun at the ceiling and hauled me to my feet.

"That's not a great way to greet someone who just saved your life," he said calmly in a deep and slightly gravelly voice. He slipped the gun from my hand, put it on safety and tucked into his belt. He gripped his broken nose and reset if with a sickening crunch. "Oh and tell lover boy he can stand down."

I looked up to see Matt standing in the isle 20 feet from us, aiming his pistol at the newcomer. I had lost him in the action and lack of air. I walked over and stood next to him.

"Who are you?" Matt asked, still not lowering his gun.

The man crossed the warehouse with a slight limp and knelt by the fallen Agent, went through his pockets, and found a phone. I tried not to look at the Agent's body. He flipped the phone open, I could see a picture of Matt and me on the tiny screen. "You called me, remember?" he said, standing up and continuing to look through the phone. "You're Matt, and you're Holly, right? And it looks like you both have been retired, just like me." He used the Agent's phone to text back to the only number programmed into it. The message was simple and untrue

-Transaction complete. The Organization would know it was untrue as soon as the bodies of the Agents were found.

"Samson," I said, finally connecting the dots. At last I got a good look at him. He was a giant, standing at about 6 foot 8 inches and all solid muscle. Samson looked like he was in his late forties, early fifties. He had short black hair streaked with gray and slight stubble. His clothes were rather plain under his bulletproof vest and tactical webbing. He seemed mostly uninjured and completely unshaken by the fight. He caught me staring and I looked away.

"Go get your things, and whatever you want off this gentleman," he told us. We didn't move. "Unless you would rather wait 'till his backup arrives," he sarcastically suggested. Matt climbed back up the shelving to get our bags and I walked over to the first fallen Agent. I pulled the ammo and goggles off him, retrieved my mother's gun and Mac10, then returned to Samson. Matt walked back and tossed me my backpack. I reloaded my Glock with the Agent's ammo and crammed the rest back into the backpack. Matt stuffed the three laser pointers he used to bluff rifle sights into his pack.

Samson, with his Remington tactical rifle in hand, led us out of the warehouse and to a waiting car in the next lot. We could hear sirens in the distance. Matt sat shotgun and I climbed into the back. We sped out of the lot and back onto the main road.

"So how did you get my number? That phone has been out of use for almost two decades," he asked.

"It was in a letter left for Holly by her mother. We were in a tight spot, thought we could use all the help we could get," Matt explained. He left out the file and the Founder. I followed his lead.

"Who is your mother?" he asked, looking in the rearview mirror at me.

"Bridget," I told him simply.

The car swerved and narrowly avoided oncoming traffic. "What? No, she never had a kid. She died around 18 years ago trying to bring the Organization down."

"I have her gun." I held up my Glock.

He glanced at my gun. "Yeah, that's it. And now that I think about it, if you were blond you could be her clone. When were you born?" he asked a little more urgently then I had expected.

"May 21, 16 years ago," I answered.

He seemed to be counting in his head for a moment. "I guess when you're out in the cold you're the last one to hear about all this. Is she...." He trailed off. I got his meaning.

"No she died in Russia, when I was six," I told him.

"We need your help," Matt prompted, trying to keep things on track.

"I owed her one, I guess I will make good on it. Damn, the woman is dead and still collecting debts. You just needed saving from the Retirement Agent, right?" he asked.

"Not exactly," I said shifting my gaze.

Samson sighed while merging onto a highway. "You are just like her," he said with a slight grin. "What do you need?" he asked, glancing back at Matt.

"We need to find a yacht, the Cicolluis. It should be in Italy or Greece," Matt told him.

Samson nodded, like that was a perfectly normal thing. He pulled a phone from his pocket and dialed. He spoke in rapid Italian and mentioned the name Cicolluis. He waited like he was on hold. After a few minutes the other person on the line came back and said something. It must have been important because Samson turned the car east and continued talking for a few more minutes. He hung up and filled us in.

"My contact said it's not in Italy. I know a guy who can smuggle us to Greece, for a fee. I don't suppose you have cash?" I shook my head no. "Of course you don't. Oh well, I can cover it. You just need to find the boat?" he asked.

"Not exactly," I said with a small grin.

"Honestly, I already regret meeting you two. What do you need with it?" he asked.

"We need to have a rather persuasive conversation with the owner," I answered, trying to sound nonchalant.

"Who's the owner?" Samson wasn't buying it.

"Our guess, the Founder." Matt said.

The car pulled off the road and onto the shoulder of the road. He turned in this seat to look at both of us. "You're screwing with me," he accused Matt.

"No, we're not." I pulled a few pages of the files out of my backpack and showed them to him.

Samson looked them over in silence for a long moment. "These are incomplete," he commented.

"We have more," I told him, but didn't move to give him the rest. We stared at each other for a moment before he merged back into traffic.

"If it is really him on the ship it's not going to be easy getting to him, let alone giving you two enough time to talk to him," he said. I could almost see the wheels in his head turning. "If I do this I will need to see the rest of the info. And I will be taking lead on this, last thing I need is some whelps making a mistake and getting me killed after all this time."

"Done," I told him. Then changed to another topic that was bugging me. "Can I ask you a question?"

"Only one? Maybe you're not as much like her as I thought," Samson replied with a smirk.

"Okay, I have several," I admitted. "What do you mean my mother was trying to bring the Organization down? She was working for them, she was legendary."

"Clearly I didn't know her as well as I had thought," he said, glancing at me as proof of that. "I knew her when we were both in, not that we worked together in the field. I was the wrecking ball the Organization used when situations got out of control, she was more like a scalpel. I left right before Epsilon died and our paths crossed when she was on her last mission. She could have turned me in, or killed me herself, but she saved me. Bridget told me she wanted the Organization taken down just as much as I did, and that she was working on something to do just that. We went our separate ways and I heard she died shortly after. That file must have been what she was working on. She was legendary alright, but that's her legacy right there in your hand."

"Why did she want them taken down?" I asked confused.

"I don't know, she never told me," he replied.

We drove for six and a half hours to Bari, stopping only for gas and a bathroom break. We found Samson's friend's fishing boat docked in Porto Nuovo. We ditched the car and snuck on board with our bags. After sneaking onto the cargo plane in the US, the fishing boat was a breeze. The boat was about 43 feet long and was painted white with teal trim. The captain and presumable Sampson's friend, was a stocky Italian man of about 35. He had a large beard and slightly bloodshot eyes. Samson's friend didn't introduce himself but showed Matt and I how to hide in the engine room. We hunkered down and waited. After about 10 minutes the boat cast off, soon we could feel the stronger rocking of the boat meaning we had hit open water. With the heat and the hum of the engines I started to doze. When the hatch to the engines was opened, I was ready for action in an instant, but relaxed when I saw Samson standing there looking unconcerned. Matt and I climbed out and joined Samson in the tiny galley.

"Let's see those files now," he said, holding out his hand. I hesitated for a second then pulled them out of my bag and passed them to him.

Matt and I sat wordlessly as Samson quickly poured over the intel, shuffling stacks and lining up pages to create a visual map of it all. He gathered the pages with the lists of possible ports on them up in his hands and pulled out his cell phone again. He made another call and read off the names of the ports to a person on the line. He waited for a minute then hung up the phone.

Sampson sat back and looked Matt and I over. "Allow an old spook to give you some unsolicited advice. In this business there are three mistakes that are perfectly fatal. The first is running to the media or a government, everything is so compartmentalized and fluid that you will never prove anything. You just end up getting yourself and some reporter killed. The second is taking on the Founder, there is a reason he is still running things after all these years. The third is falling in love. Using your loved one as leverage is what they do best," he said gravely.

"But you took on the Organization and are doing it again, and some of the other agents even have families," I said confused.

He smirked at my words. "I never said it was fatal for the agent. They killed my wife and unborn child, they killed your mother eventually and someday they will come for the other agents' families too. Someone always ends up in a body bag, that is, if there is enough of a body to put in the bag," he explained darkly. "And you both are making two of those mistakes. Keep your mouth shut, do as you're told, mind your own business, and love nothing, them's the rules. But if you follow that, you live as their blind puppet the rest of your life and die anyway. The Organization needs to fall, I am just giving you a heads-up on how it will end. After everything is said and done, I am in the wind again, all debts paid". With that he got up and left the galley. Matt and I sat in silence for a moment.

I took Matt by the hand and walked with him to the bow of the boat. We stood in the wind and watched the moon reflecting off the water. Finally I turned to him and said "There seems to be a conflict of interests, he wants the Founder dead, we want him alive so that we can get back in".

"You want back in. We could just kill the Founder and disappear too," he said just loud enough for me to hear over the wind.

"Is that what you really want?" I asked him, watching how his eyes caught the light off the water.

"I want to be with you. I don't see why you want to be an agent so badly. The life sucks. You are the brightest thing in it for me," he told me brushing my hair out of my face.

"All I have ever wanted for as long as I can remember is to be a legendary agent like her. It's stupid, I know, but I just can't forget her," I explained poorly.

"No, I get it. I lost a parent at six, too, you know. And when my mom died I got revenge. All that is over for me, but you're still not done with yours. I know how loss like that gets into your head. All I am saying is I am here for you. As long as it takes for you to find your way out and finish it, I will be right here." He laced his fingers with mine. "I won't let go". He leaned his face down to mine and I held my breath.

We were interrupted by the captain of the boat yelling out the window in Italian. We didn't understand it but it sounded important. Hand in hand we walked back to the galley and found Sampson finishing a hurried phone conversation.

"...Yeah, two long packs, three standards- no wait scratch that, a wet pack and three com. packs. No, I got the rest." He paused to listen and we sat down. "No, I needed them an hour ago. I called you because you're fast, clean and quiet". We could hear a voice on the line but couldn't make it out. He finished with a curt, "Thanks," and hung up, then addressed us. "Alright, I am used to last-minute operations and no funding, but you two are starting to become expensive. My buddy found the ship, it's docked for now, but it won't be there for long. One more night at most. At this point we are just waiting on the equipment I just ordered. We will dock and I will go pick it all up. There are bunks through there, get some shut eye, you will need it."

I dragged my backpack through the door he indicated and found a bedroom with a bunk bed. I opened what I thought was a closet and found the smallest bathroom I had ever seen. I could barely fit inside with my backpack. After a quick and mostly cold shower, I changed and collapsed on the top bunk. I could hear hushed voices back in the galley.

"How sure are you that the girl isn't just using you?" Sampson's deep gravelly voice carried.

"Using me? No way," Matt replied.

"Don't get all upset. I am just saying if she is really like her mom, then people, particularly men, are disposable. I have seen the look in an agent's eyes when they are in this game for love, you got it. She doesn't seem to. Maybe there is something else that she is after," he suggested.

"She is not her mother," Matt retorted.

"Fine. Sorry I said anything. She is probably done changing by now, you should go". His footsteps faded away. The dark room was slashed for a moment by a stream of light from the galley, then went dark again as Matt entered. He stepped into the bathroom, but I fell asleep before he turned on the shower. I started to dream.

I was sitting next to my mother on a ferry, watching the waves roll by. I was about 5 years old.

"Exits?" my mother asked calmly. It was a game we played.

"But we are on a boat, mommy," I said confused. The normal rules didn't fit for boats.

"Try," she said, stroking my hair, brushing it out of my eyes.

I looked around and thought, frowning with the effort. "umm, back there, the exit sign. Umm, oh and the stairs." I smiled, I was winning the game.

"That's two, you need three to win," she said, holding up three fingers to illustrate her point.

"The water?" I asked.

She smiled her dazzling smile. "I guess that counts," she kissed my forehead. "You win."

I woke up as the boat gently bumped into something. I looked out the porthole and saw that we had docked. Rolling off the top bunk, I landed as softly as I could, but woke Matt up anyway.

"Looks like we made port," I told him as he stretched. "I am going topside".

"Right behind you," Matt said.

We slipped shoes on and made our way to the aft deck. The captain was leaning against the railing smoking a cigarette and coiling line. He nodded in greeting, which we returned. I took a minute to look around. Sampson was nowhere to be seen. Early morning sun shown off the water. Our boat was in a small harbor, docked alongside seven others, another six were tied on the opposite side of the dock. My eyes scanned the names on each, none were the Cicolluis. I could see a barge being towed into a separate dock, a little further away. On shore a wide road divided the docks from the bright white buildings beyond. I counted three cars parked by the road. There was little movement anywhere, it looked like the place was still waking up. I mimed food to the captain, he gave a unconcerned wave of the hand and dropped his cigarette butt in the water to put it out. Matt and I returned to the galley and dug around till we found canned fruit and a few eggs. After breakfast we repacked our bags, cleaned our guns and lent a hand to the captain with small chores. The language barrier was a bit of a problem, we ended up doing a lot of miming and pointing. By noon Sampson still hadn't shown, the captain didn't seem to know where he had gone, or cared. Matt and I stopped for a quick lunch of canned soup. The captain grabbed a bottle of red wine from a cabinet, uncorked it, and took it with him as he cleaned and repaired fishnets. Hours later he had finished his liquid lunch and Sampson returned carrying several bags. He brought them into the galley and set them on the table.

"The Cicolluis is docked two miles east," he informed us without bothering to greet anyone. "This," he said opening the bags, "is the finest equipment I can buy last minute without government or military affiliation."

The bags contained two sniper rifles with sights, ammo, two standard radios and headsets, one waterproof headset, a tiny air tank and mouthpiece, and a tightly rolled up dry suit with tactical webbing to hold equipment, fins and a mask.

We set up and prepped our equipment as the sun set. Everyone could feel it, this was the calm before the storm.

Chapter 19

At dusk, we were suited up and moving into position. Sampson had taken one of the rifles and one radio headset and disappeared into the dark. Matt held the other rifle on his lap as he steered the captain's tiny dingy out of the harbor and around the rock jetty, closer to the Cicolluis. I sat next to him, strapping equipment to my tactical webbing on the dry suit. Matt stopped the tiny boat just outside of the port where the Cicolluis, and hopefully, the Founder was. We bobbed in the unprotected waters. Wordlessly I undid the clasp on the silver locket around my neck, I held it for a second then pressed it into Matt's hand.

"Keep this safe for me," I said. I tried to read his face but it was too dark, the moon was hidden by clouds that night.

Matt nodded. "Come back to me". He said it with just a bit of plea in his voice. He cupped my cheek in his palm and we kissed. The moment was broken by Sampson over the radio.

"I am in place, it's time," his voice crackled slightly over the radio.

I stole a glance at Matt then arched my back and slipped head-first into the water. The coolness of the water cleared my mind. I oriented myself and put the air tank's mouthpiece to my lips. One breath later I was off, swimming at a natural pace towards the huge ship's white hull. Once I had reached it, I paused. I pressed a button on my waterproof headset, sending a beep to both Matt and Sampson. Sampson sent two beeps back, signaling it was all clear.

I kicked gently to bring myself closer to the surface. A porthole window and the railings on the first deck above came into view, no one was there. I swam around the back of the yacht and pulled myself onto the swim deck. Watching the roatation of the guard I crept to a porthole on the starboard side. A double beep came across the radio, so far so good. I peered into the window just inside the railing. I saw an office with a large desk, chairs and a seating area just beyond. It was dark and the door was closed. I pulled a magnet from one of the many pouches on my tactical wet suit. Ever so slowly I touched the magnet to the sensor on the window. The little light on the frame of the window stayed green. I pulled a roll of tape from another pocket and taped the magnet in place. Praying that the window didn't squeak, I slid it open. The light stayed green the whole time. Feet first, I slid inside and closed the window behind me. My heart was pounding, I made it in. I looked around the room again, let out the breath I was holding. The room smelled of cigar smoke and reminded me of the LA Local Director's office. The room had a masculine and wealthy look to it. Every surface was immaculate. In the weak light that came in through the window behind me I scanned for traps, sensors, hidden weapons or other forms of danger.

A light came on in the far corner of the room, making me jump and I drew my weapon.

"Hello, Hanna," came a deep calm voice.

Illuminated by the ornate lamp on the polished wooden table was a man sitting in a wing backed chair. I had missed him because of the darkness of the corner of the room. He was about 50 with black hair peppered with gray. He wore a perfectly tailored three-piece gray suit with a silk tie and matching pocket square. His clean shaven, handsome face was lined with age.

"Put that gun away, we wouldn't be in the same hemisphere if I didn't want to talk to you," he said with a relaxed but authoritative tone.

I lowered my Glock but didn't holster it. "You know my name, but I don't know yours," I replied, faking a calm to match his. My heart was drumming its way out of my chest.

"I have several, such is the nature of this business. You may call me Founder, Joseph King or Father, if you should so desire." He slowly opened a polished wooden box on the table at his elbow and withdrew a cigar, clipped it, lit it and took a long pull.

"Father?" I asked taken by surprise.

"Yes, your mother, Alison, and I were married briefly. But, it's a long story and we have limited time. Let's keep useless questions to a minimum," King said with the air of someone explaining nuclear physics to a child.

"Liar." It was all I could manage. It didn't make sense. My mother worked for the Organization, then hated them and tried to take them down, we ended up on the run. How did the Founder work into the whole thing?

Rather than being offended, King cracked a bemused grin. "Isn't it funny how when you're raised in a world of lies, you have such a hard time finding the truth, even when it's right in front of you."

"If you're the Founder then prove it, reinstate Matt and me," I challenged.

"Happily, for a price." He took another pull from his cigar. "I propose a threefold trade. You get information, I tell you all about the Organization, who and why Matt was burned and everything you want to know about your mother and myself. In exchange you give me the files you found, report everything you found out and how."

"What's in it for Matt?" I asked cautiously.

"Reinstatement … and you. That's why we put you as his partner. We saw that he wasn't afraid of us exposing what he did in the United States anymore and we needed new leverage. He loves you, and as long as he does, we have him," King answered.

"You can't make people fall in love," I replied. My head was already spinning.

"No, of course not, but then again you're not his first partner. We knew he would fall sooner or later if we kept matching him with his type," King said with a shrug.

I wanted to gape at him but I hid my surprise. Not Matt's first partner? I mentally shook myself, I had to stay focused.

"Think about it, you get reinstated. I will even throw in a bonus, Sampson walks free. All you have to do is listen," he said.

"What's the catch?" I asked suspiciously.

"By the end of this you will be begging me to let you on a special assignment to help take down a little problem of mine," King said. He was baiting me.

"What problem?" I asked, knowing I was taking the bait.

"It's the same problem your mother ran into all those years ago. I thought I had taken care of if after she had left, but I made a mistake. My house is not in order as I often pretend it is. But, let me start from the beginning. Have a seat, my dear daughter." He indicated the chair across from him.

My radio cracked to life in my ear. "Don't do it, Holly, we won't be able to cover you from that angle" warned Sampson.

"Oh, and you will have to turn off your mic. What I am about to tell you cannot be allowed to leak," King added.

I thought about it for a split second, then turned my mic off, but remained standing, still holding my Glock. My Father acknowledged this as good enough and began to tell an earth shattering story.

"I left the CIA what feels like a lifetime ago, fed up with their red tape and inability to act fast enough to make a bigger difference. I started my own empire with one goal: peace. Billions of dollars are being made from profiting from war, but why not peace? Divisions of my empire attack and overthrow drug lords, end gang wars, stop pipelines of human trafficking and prevent and react to terrorism."

"But why not tell all the agents that we are fighting for peace?" I asked confused.

"Because we let them think that they are fighting for whatever is most important to that agent, whether its money, patriotism, or a loved one. Love and fear are stronger motivators than peace," he explained, then continued with his story.

"The problem arose when I discovered factions inside my empire. One that I have dubbed The Coup, doesn't believe in my vision of peace. They have been causing trouble and desperately seek to kill me. The other faction is the True Believers, self-named, they believe in my goal but have their own ways of accomplishing peace. Both are hiding inside my empire. Every time I catch one, another operation is taken over by another radical. I can't find all of them and killing everyone I suspect would cripple my empire. Which is where your mother comes in. The Coup killed her partner, Epsilon, so that she would be willing to take a new assignment. They chose five agents to investigate five members of core management. The rest of my empire didn't know which of the five is the Founder. I had a mole in the department that I thought would try something like that. He told me they planned to send undercover agents into the management's lives and try to find out who was the Founder, then kill the Founder so that The Coup could take over. I looked over the list and told my mole to put your mother on my case. I liked her the best. If I had to be investigated then it was going to be by a beautiful woman. Weeks later your mother just so happened to start to frequent my favorite coffee shop."

"You picked her out?" I scoffed. The truth that the Organization was not as stable as it looked was not that shocking, but I had always dreamed about how my parents met. A mission was not what I had imagined.

"I didn't think we would fall in love, I expected her to look into my life for a month or so then report back that she had found nothing and disappear. She was more charming then I expected and much more beautiful in person then her picture led me to believe. I fell for her, and I like to believe that she truly loved me in return. I proposed to her after three months. We were married after another two months. I never forgot what had brought her into my life and I was careful to keep her in the dark, but we were happy. One night I came home and she was holding a pregnancy test. I was overjoyed, but she was just shocked. The next night we were laying in bed when she got a call. She took it on the balcony. She came back in, she set the phone down and just stared at me. I asked her what was wrong and she told me she knew that I was the Founder, but didn't report it to her handler. I told her I knew that she was sent to kill me but none of it mattered. We argued and she left that night. She was just trying to keep you safe. Hanna was the name I picked out. I found her handler and traced the orders to the source, I thought killing him would end The Coup. I was wrong. They found your mother and wanted to use her again, knowing that I would do anything to keep you both safe. The True Believers eventually caught up to you and your mother as well. The TB thought that because you could be used as leverage that it was too big of a risk to let you both live. They coordinated the attack in Russia. I sent an independent and trusted agent to verify what had happened. He found two burned bodies in the morgue and everyone thought you both were dead. That week a little girl entered Boarding School, but so did 13 others. You were lost in the system for years." My head was spinning and King took another long pull from his cigar, then continued. I watched the smoke curl up towards the ceiling, barely breathing.

"Until The Coup heard a rumor you were still alive and had become a trainee. They set up abductions of young trainees trying to find someone who matched your description. Normal forces agents rescued the kids and called the whole mess a training exercise. Your name leaked though the network and a TB agent figured they had another shot and eliminated a possible threat to me. They couldn't just kill an agent without a reason so they snuck into the LA LCC and killed the Local Director," he explained.

"But they made a mistake, they used Matt's gun and not mine," I said putting the pieces together.

"Exactly, they were hoping that you would get killed by a Retirement Agent, in spite of their mistake. But a Coup agent replaced the Retirement Agent, with another agent with orders to find files that Bridget had hidden because they contained intel on me, then capture or kill you and Matt."

"Which is why two teenage agents survived an encounter with a so-called Retirement Agent," I said, glad that we hadn't been facing the real thing.

"Precisely. It seems you have been hunted your whole life," King said with a nod.

"So what now? If we go back, won't they just kill me or try to use me again?" I asked.

"Did you ever have a chance to play chess with your mother growing up?" he asked.

"Yes, why?" I said, confused as to how this was relevant.

"Your mother was one of the greatest players I have ever known. If she had taught you well you would see that you have always been a pawn. Protecting that aptly-named King is the goal of the chess player, but a pawn can survive if placed in exactly the right position and then distracting the opponent's attention with a more pressing threat. Don't fear, either way I will win the game of chess and you will help me," he explained with a self-satisfied smirk. He rose from his chair, pulled a small torn piece of paper from his pocket and pressed it into my hand.

"If my calculations are correct, my security and backup security will be fighting The Coup operatives that you unwittingly lead to my door any second. I suggest you leave now to avoid getting caught in the crossfire." He kissed my forehead, I was too shocked to react. He gently pushed me towards the window before he moved calmly behind the desk and pulled a uzi from under the desk. "My people will collect you after dealing with the Coup for debrief and reinstatement. Till then..." He checked the clip and cocked the gun. "Keep your head down, my darling".

I seemed to come up from a fog and found myself moving towards the window. With a flick of a switch, I turned the mic back on. "Guys, we might have company closing in on the yacht," I advised, tucking the paper inside the watertight suit.

"Holly! Finally, get your ass out of there. I've got three speed boats closing in. You're about to be hit, hard." Sampson said urgently. I could hear gunfire on the far side of the boat and by the bow.

I slid open the window and pulled myself through. I straightened up for a second, looking for Matt and the dingy for a quick exit. Gunfire rang out again. I fell oddly, on my side. Then rolled under the railing and hit the water. Without bothering with the air tank I kicked hard for the spot where Matt had anchored the dingy. My lungs were screaming without air, but I was so focused on getting to Matt that I blocked everything else out. It was too dark to see the black of the dingy's hull among the rocks and black underside of the dock.

Hands reached into the water and pulled me to the surface. I gulped air and registered that it was Matt. I tried to help pull myself into the tiny boat but my arm didn't work right. I ended up collapsing in a heap between bench seats. My brain seemed to be running on slow motion. Matt was swearing and holding a wad of cloth to me. I tried to brush him off and sit up, but he held me down. We didn't have time for whatever this was, we had to get away from the fire fight.

"Damn it, Holly, hold this over your shoulder or you'll bleed out!" he yelled.

My mind cleared with a sudden start like an electric shock. My shoulder radiated pain through my whole body. I accepted the cloth and tried to stem the blood flow. Now it made sense, I fell oddly on the yacht because I had taken a stray bullet. I was in shock until then and was able to swim with a hole in my shoulder. Matt turned to the tiny motor and steered us out of the port and back to the fishing boat in the next harbor. Every wave we bounced over sent a new wave of pain through my body. I gritted my teeth and willed myself not to cry. The captain was waiting for us, he helped haul me out of the dingy and onto the dock. Once on the deck the captain hooked the dingy to his boat and cast off. Within minutes he had left us on the dock and was going as fast as he could without drawing attention. Matt collected our bags that the captain had left sitting on the dock under a pile of rope. My breath came in ragged gasps. Matt carried both backpacks and half dragged me down the docks and into an alleyway across the road I had studied upon arrival. He lowered me to the ground while he decided what to do. We could still hear the gunshot from the yacht. I tried to explain that we were back in and they would be coming to reinstate us, soon but it was hard to talk. Matt was at my side in a heartbeat and covered my hand holding the cloth with his, adding pressure. He said something, but I didn't understand. I held his free hand. We did it, we met the Founder and would be reinstated. We survived the civil war that was raging inside the Organization. I was in arms of the man I loved. My vision tunneled and I blacked out.

Epilogue

I was out for what happened next, but I pieced it together from reports. Matt held me and tried to figure out where the closest hospital was when the agents my father had sent surrounded the alley. He knew he couldn't shoot his way out with me so wounded. He surrendered and they took us in. They patched me up and debriefed us both. The bullet did less damage then I thought, I was in a sling for a week and would make a full recovery. I was ordered to do some physical therapy for my shoulder and I would have quite the scar, but I would be fine. I told Matt everything my father had said. He told me about his first partner. We were told we were still agents, but would have a new handler, appointed by someone named King, because there was still some bad blood between me and Tonya. The files that were in my backpack went back to the Organization to be analyzed then destroyed. I was able to keep the letters from my mother, her gun, the picture of us and the locket. Matt was able to keep his gun as well. The whole process took three weeks.

After all of that we packed up our few belongings and were put on a cargo plane to our new location. We were told that we would be attached to a new task force that was already set up there. On the plane I thought over everything that my father had said and realized that he was wrong about one thing, he had said that by the end of it all I would be begging to help fight in the factions inside the Organization. I have had more than enough of that mess for one life time. I smiled to myself. Maybe he was not as good a chess player as he thought he was. I held Matt's hand for the ride and tucked my hand into my pocket. I felt a piece of paper and pulled it out. Through all of the commotion I had forgotten the paper that my father had pressed into my hand. I read what he had written across the front.

Check, your move.

But it was what was written on the back that made my blood run cold. Damn, he was good. With that one phrase I was back in, willing to do whatever it took.

Your mother is still alive.